Emily can't play today...

Emily pushed them away, snarling like an angry dog.

"Look at her teeth," Sarah whispered to Tim.

"I know."

Emily's teeth were long and pointed, and her eyes were cold and glittering as she watched them suspiciously. Her face was almost as pale as the white sheet she lay on, and although she was weak, she recoiled from the garlic violently. Her eyes flashed furiously at them whenever they came close with it.

Other Bullseye Books you will enjoy

My sister, the Vampire

BY
NANCY
GARDEN

Bullseye Books • Alfred A. Knopf • New York

Special thanks to Barbara Seuling,
who suggested some magic tricks

To certain persistent Vermont bats:
You know who you are!
and
for the Romankis:
Angela, Simon, Nicola, Janice, and George

A BULLSEYE BOOK PUBLISHED BY ALFRED A. KNOPF, INC.
Text copyright © 1992 by Nancy Garden
Cover art copyright © 1992 by Dave Henderson

Library of Congress Cataloging-in-Publication Data
Garden, Nancy.
My sister, the vampire / by Nancy Garden.
p.   cm.
"Bullseye books."
Summary: A beautiful Maine summer turns deadly for Sarah, Tim, and
Jenny Hoskins and their neighbors as they discover the horrifying
truth about the strange new owners of Spool Island.
ISBN 0-679-82659-9 (pbk.) — ISBN 0-679-92659-3 (lib. bdg.)
[1. Vampires—Fiction.   2. Brothers and sisters—Fiction.
3. Horror stories.]   I. Title.
PZ7.G165 Mx   1992
[Fic]—dc20   91-32580
RL: 5.4
First Bullseye Books edition: September 1992

Contents

chapter 1

"We'll Be Good!"

The icy water swirled around his legs as he dove through it and emerged yards ahead of the other swimmers . . .

"OUCH!" Tim Hoskins yelled indignantly, punched rudely back into reality by his sister Sarah. He put down the suitcase he'd just carried up the path to his family's summer cabin in Starfish Harbor, Maine. The cabin was right on the water, so, as Mr. Hoskins often said, it had a little of everything—at least both woods and ocean.

"Stop daydreaming. Mom wants to say something," Sarah told him, shifting her butterfly collection from one arm to the other. Sarah was thir-

1

teen, one year older than Tim, and inclined to be bossy.

Their mother looked at him gravely. "I was just asking you and Sarah to remember," she said, "that you're responsible for Jenny and Tink while Dad and I are at Grandpa's. Especially until Aunt Clara gets here . . ."

"That should be by tonight," Dad said as he pushed Tim's ten-speed bike up the path to the cabin.

"We'll be fine," said Tim, taking the bike and wishing his parents would leave so he could go out for a run. He was training for the Iron Boy Triathlon: a half-mile swim, a ten-mile bike race, and a three-mile run, to be held in October on Cape Cod, Massachusetts. Tim had a good chance of placing, according to his coach at school—*if* he kept up his training all summer.

"Sure we will." Sarah poked their five-year-old sister Jenny. "Won't we?"

Jenny had one arm around the family's black Labrador retriever, Champion Tinkerfield Coreopsis, otherwise known as Tink. She looked doubtful, but she nodded dutifully. "And you'll make Grandpa all better," she said. "Huh, Mommy?"

Tim saw his parents exchange worried glances. "We'll try, kittycat," Mom said, hugging Jenny. But Tim knew enough about strokes to know that it would take more than Mom's good sense and Dad's cheerfulness to make their grandfather better. Grandpa couldn't move or speak, Mom had told them last night when the phone call came saying he was in the hospital. The Hoskinses had still been home in Boston then, packing for their summer in Maine. But now just the kids and Tink would stay in the cabin, with Aunt Clara when she came, for as long as Mr. and Mrs. Hoskins were needed further north.

"There's a couple more things in the car," Dad said briskly. "Sarah, I think I saw your Dracula scrapbook on the back seat. And Tim, you might just give me a hand with the groceries."

In ten more minutes, the Hoskinses' station wagon was empty of everything except the suitcase Mr. and Mrs. Hoskins were taking with them, and the groceries were more or less put away. Mrs. Hoskins called everyone into what the family called the Big Room. The cabin was basically just one large space that was living room and dining room combined. The tiny kitchen was off the Big Room, and there was a porch outside. Upstairs were the bathroom and a few under-the-eaves-type bedrooms, reached by a spiral staircase.

"Well," said Mom awkwardly, "I guess this is it. We'll call often to let you know how things are."

"And we want you to have a good time anyway," Dad said. "I know that's what Grandpa would want. There's no point in spoiling your summer, he'd say.

There's . . ." Mr. Hoskins's voice cracked a little and he cleared his throat. "So that means going on just as if we were here—Tim with your training, Sarah with your butterflies . . ."

"And the garden," added Mom. "If you could weed it, both of you . . ."

"Me too," said Jenny.

Mom smiled. "*All* of you. Sorry, kittycat. And of course"—she glanced at Dad—"you'll do whatever Aunt Clara says."

Tim tried not to groan out loud, but Sarah did, and made a face, too. He knew what she was thinking: Schedules. The last time their great-aunt had taken care of them, she'd planned each day so carefully that there wasn't any time left over to *do* anything. Tim hadn't been able to train properly, and Sarah had had to neglect her worm farm. That had been her last year's passion, along with Dracula, the Wolf Man, and any horror movie she could see. Aunt Clara had limited their moviegoing, though, to things like *Cinderella* and *David Copperfield*.

"We'll be good," said Jenny piously, her blond curls bobbing up and down as she nodded. Tim liked her, but sometimes he wanted to shake her.

"I know you will," Mom said. "I've told Aunt Clara that you're still good friends with John and Emily Gibson, so she'll expect you to spend at least some time with them. And I've told her she can always call on Mr. and Mrs. Gibson if anything goes wrong." She looked around the Big Room and smiled bravely. "That's that. We're all set, I think."

"I guess," said Dad. "C'mere, family." He spread his arms wide and gathered them all in, even Tink, and everyone said goodbye. Then Mr. and Mrs. Hoskins got into the station wagon and drove away, while the children waved them off from the yard.

And then, inside, the phone rang.

chapter 2

Freedom

"You go," said Tim.

"No, you," said Sarah.

"I'll get it," Jenny announced, and ran into the cabin.

A moment later she popped out again with a funny expression on her face. "It's Aunt Clara," she called. "She wants Mommy."

Tim and Sarah looked at each other, and then Sarah took charge as usual, marching importantly into the house. Tim followed.

"Yes," Sarah was saying. "Oh, no!" (That was her insincere voice, Tim knew.) "That's awful! Does it hurt a lot? . . . No, Mom and Dad just left. . . . Yes, sure we'll be fine. . . . Yes, the Gibsons live pretty close. . . . Sure. . . . Oh . . . no, they haven't got a phone." (Tim was momentarily startled at that, but then he saw that Sarah had crossed her fingers.) "But we'll tell them. . . . Yes. Please feel better. And don't worry. Goodbye."

"Well?" Tim prompted eagerly when she'd hung up. "Well?"

Sarah grabbed him by his hands and pranced around in a circle, whirling him with her. "She had an accident!" she shouted gleefully. "She smashed up her car. She sprained her knee and bumped her head. And she CAN'T COME! Yippee!"

"Wow!" Visions of a wonderful summer renewed themselves in Tim's head. Now he wouldn't have to worry about his training schedule. Aunt Clara talked a lot about "a healthy mind in a healthy body," but it was the healthy mind part that interested her more.

"Aunt Clara's not coming?" said Jenny, her lower lip trembling a little. Jenny was still young enough to like the structure Aunt Clara provided.

"No, Jen, she can't," Sarah explained. "At least not for a while. She has to stay in the hospital for a few days, while her knee and the bump on her head get better. And then"—Sarah turned to Tim—"she has to get her car fixed, or buy a new one, so . . ."

"So it could be weeks before she can come, right?" Tim asked.

"Well, maybe not weeks. But days anyway.

7

Someone's starting to fix the car already, she said. But—"

"I want Mommy," wailed Jenny.

Sarah went down on her knees to her. "No, you don't," she said. "You said last night you were going to be a big girl about that."

"I want Aunt Clara then."

"No one wants Aunt Clara," Sarah said coldly.

"I do," insisted Jenny tearfully.

"Now look at what you've done," Tim said to Sarah. He gave Jenny a hug. "Jenny, I know you like Aunt Clara, but what's wrong with me and Sarah? Hmm? We're going to have a great time, just the three of us and Tink."

Jenny shook her head, pouting. "No, we're not. You're always on your bike or running, and Sarah's always reading about vampires or playing with her worms . . ."

"Butterflies," Sarah corrected. "Worms was last summer."

"You never play with me," Jenny said.

"We will this time." Tim poked Sarah. "We promise."

"Right," said Sarah. "We promise. Now, how about we all make the beds and then finish unpacking and then go out and look for butterflies?"

"How about," said Tim, "I go out for a run while you and Jenny look for butterflies? Then we'll make the beds and unpack."

"Okay," Sarah agreed amiably. "Just so I get my butterflies."

"Just so I get my run," said Tim. "Fair's fair."

"Right," Sarah called as Tim headed up the stairs to change into his running shorts and shoes. "And we're going to take turns with Jenny, right?"

"Oh, right," said Tim. "Of course. Sure."

But out on the quiet country road, with his feet flying along the pavement and his head tossed back in the wind he created, he wasn't so sure about taking turns. It wasn't that he minded looking after Jenny once in a while; she could even be fun when she wasn't whiny. It was just that Sarah's idea of taking turns usually didn't mean sharing fifty-fifty. When it comes to jobs, it's more like seventy-five–twenty-five, he mused, with her having the twenty-five and me the seventy-five. . . .

It was too nice a day to think about that, though. He shut his mind off and just ran, enjoying the cool air and his own speed. By the time he turned back, deciding to run down the other side of the point, where the Gibsons lived, he felt cheerful and ready for anything.

"Tim!"

Ordinarily, Tim resented being interrupted on a run, but that was John Gibson's voice. And there, he realized, was the Gibsons' house. It was on the right-hand branch of the road that went down the

9

point; the Hoskinses lived on the left-hand branch. There was also a short path through the woods connecting the two houses, and the distance between them that way was a lot less than it was by the road.

Tim slowed to a jog and came up in front of John, who was leaning on his battered bike and smiling broadly.

"You're back!" John said, his sandy hair flopping over his sunburned, freckled face. "When did you get here?"

"Oh, about an hour ago."

"I've been waiting."

"Sorry I didn't write or anything."

John's smile deepened into a grin. "You say that every summer. Sorry I didn't either."

"You say *that* every summer. So how are things?"

"Okay. Well, sort of okay. You want to walk? You're all sweaty; you shouldn't just stop, should you?"

"No," admitted Tim. "Thanks." He started walking, and John pushed his bike along beside him, his wide, handsome face still grinning. His thick mane of hair was, if anything, longer and bushier than it had been last fall when the Hoskinses had left.

"You training for that thing?" John asked. His voice, Tim noticed with envy, was deeper, too.

"That tri-whatever that you told me about last summer?"

"Triathlon," said Tim. "Yep. You still doing magic?"

"Yeah. Gibson the Great at your service." John gave Tim a deep bow, ending with a flourish. "Hey, I'm doing a show tomorrow! I've been performing at birthday parties since March. It's fun and I get paid for it. Maybe you and Sarah and Jenny could come. It's just a little kids' party, but you might get some laughs out of it."

"Sure. You must be getting good if you get paid."

John chuckled. "I still can't do the rabbit-and-hat trick, though."

Tim laughed, remembering last year when John had stuffed a terrified rabbit of his twelve-year-old sister's into the special hiding place he had for things that were supposed to appear out of thin air. But by the time he was ready to pretend to pull it out of his dad's old top hat, the rabbit had run away.

"How's everything?" Tim asked.

"The dock survived the winter," John said, "and our boat's fine. Dad's still lobstering, and I go out with him pretty often. But Emily's sick, and that's kind of weird."

"Weird? How come?"

"You know how she loves her pet rabbits? Well, she keeps having these crazy dreams about them.

11

The first time, she woke up crying and babbling. We couldn't figure out what was wrong, but later she said she had rabbits all over her bed. Now she keeps talking about this one big one. I mean, I know she raises rabbits and all, but you'd think she could forget about them when she's asleep! She hasn't been eating much lately either, and Mom makes her stay in bed a lot because she's so weak she's fainted a couple of times. The doctor's giving her iron pills, but he's not sure they'll help. Otherwise, things are pretty much the same. Maybe Emily'll perk up when she sees Sarah. Unless Sarah's still collecting worms. Emily never did like that too much."

"It's butterflies now," Tim told him. "She's even stopped collecting Dracula stuff, though she still has that scrapbook."

"She'd better not bring it over. It really freaked Emily last summer."

"Then it's a good thing we weren't here last Halloween. Remember the year we *were* here for it and Sarah scared Emily by dressing up as a ghost and moaning outside her window? Last year would've been even worse. Sarah was still into Dracula then. You should've seen her. My sister, the vampire."

John groaned appreciatively. "Teeth and all?"

"Teeth and all."

The boys grinned at each other. Then John

slapped Tim on the back. "Hey, it's good you're back! Maybe we could all go out to the islands in the dinghy Saturday if Dad's not using it. How about we go for a picnic?"

"Great," said Tim, gladder now than ever that Aunt Clara wouldn't be coming. "Maybe we could go out to Spool Island again . . ."

"Horseshoe," said John. "And Hedgehog, but not Spool."

"Why not?"

"Someone's bought it. Some city fellow with a funny name. He's put up No Trespassing signs. Keeps to himself, so no one knows him, and Dad says the rumor is that he's kind of crazy. But the other islands would be fine."

"Okay," said Tim. "It's a date."

"Don't you have to ask your folks?"

"Nope." And Tim told John about his grandfather and Aunt Clara. By the time he left, they had a ninety-eight percent firm date for Saturday—he, Sarah, and Jenny (Emily was too sick, John said)— assuming John's dad didn't need the dinghy.

Maybe, Tim thought, running out to the end of the point on the Gibsons' side, this year I can get John to row the dinghy alongside when I'm swimming. Coach said I should have someone do that if I do any cold-water training. And I really should; it's not going to be exactly warm off Cape Cod in October, even if it'll be a lot warmer than it is here.

Wish we had a boat, he thought, after reaching the end of the point and running back up to the fork. Funny about Emily. But she always was a little wimpy. Sarah's too bossy, but at least she's got some spunk to her. Don't know what she sees in Emily; Em's so—so sort of princessy.

He turned into his own driveway just in time to hear a bloodcurdling scream coming from the cabin.

chapter 3

Bat-in-the-Box

Tim tore into the cabin. The screams seemed to be coming from the second floor, and they were accompanied by loud barks.

Jenny intercepted him at the foot of the spiral staircase. "Mices, mices," she chortled, pointing upward. "Mices that fly! Sarah can't move!" She giggled wildly, apparently enjoying herself—or maybe enjoying the spectacle of an out-of-commission Sarah.

Tim took the stairs two at a time and burst into the small room Sarah and Jenny shared. Sarah was sitting on the floor in one corner, shaking, her eyes on a small black object, rather like a damp, very dirty dishrag, that hung at the window, suspended

15

from the curtain rod. Tink was standing stiff-legged nearby, barking his head off.

"What in . . ." Tim began. Then it hit him, and he felt himself smirk. "It's just a bat, Sar'," he said, not unkindly, peering at it with interest. "Where'd you find it?"

Sarah extended a trembling finger toward her closet.

"Yeah?" Tim said and reached for the door. "I wonder how come—"

"Don't!" Sarah shouted. "There are more."

Tim paused. "How many more? Shut *up*, Tink." He grabbed Tink's collar and yanked him back, but Tink went right on barking.

"I don't know. Two or three. Four or five." Sarah gradually unfolded herself from the floor, keeping a wary eye on the bat. "What are we going to do, Tim?"

"We'll think of something. I guess we should try to catch them and put them outside. If we're going to stay here alone, we can't let ourselves be beaten by a few bats." He eyed the curtain-rod bat dubiously, wondering if it would bite if he tried to capture it.

"Oh, sure," said Sarah. "Just grab at them with our bare hands, right? Bats carry disease; I did a science report on them."

"Well, maybe not bare hands," Tim said. "How about cardboard boxes? We've got plenty of those."

16

"They'll fly right out again."

Tim's eyes scanned the room and lit on Sarah's butterfly net. "How about that?" he asked. "If a butterfly can't get out of it, I'm pretty sure a bat couldn't."

"My *net?*" said Sarah. "My beautiful new NET? Not on your life!"

"Then I guess we'd better just let the bats stay." Tim shoved Tink out into the hall and slammed the door shut. "I don't think they'll make very noisy roommates."

"The bats," said Sarah, "are not staying."

"I don't know what you're so upset about." Tim sat down on Sarah's bed. "Last year at this time, if I remember right, you were practicing your vampire act for Halloween. It's probably just one of your old friends."

"Very funny," Sarah said. "Vampires are make-believe. For your information, Timothy Daniel Hoskins, these bats are real. Hi, Jenny."

Jenny had opened the door and stuck her head in. Tink squeezed past her. "Mices?" Jenny inquired.

"No, Jenny," Tim said gently. "Not mice, bats."

Tink took up his post at the window, barking, a little hoarsely now.

Jenny settled herself comfortably beside Tim on Sarah's bed. "What's a bat?"

Tim looked at Sarah.

"A bat," Sarah said, glancing anxiously from the window to the closet and back again, "is a sort of a—well, it's not a mouse, and it's not a bird, but it's sort of like both of them rolled into one. It flies around a lot."

Jenny stared at the bat in the window. "That one doesn't fly."

"Oh, yes, it does, Jenny," said Sarah. "It flew right out of our closet and into my hair. Yuck!" She shuddered.

"Oh, come on, Sarah," Tim said. "That's just a *story* about bats. Bats don't really do that."

"Oh, no? Watch this." Sarah took a ruler from the little table that served as a desk, and, holding it gingerly at arm's length, poked the bat. With a squeak, the bat let go of the curtain rod and flew twice around the room, swooping low on each circuit, and coming very close to the tops of their heads. Tink danced crazily after it, snapping and leaping, but it stayed just out of reach.

"YEEEOOOW!" screamed Jenny, and ran to Sarah, who was now standing in the middle of the room with her eyes closed.

Tim dove for the net, swooped at the bat just as the bat swooped at him, and—

"Got it!" he said triumphantly, twisting the top of the net closed.

"My net!" cried Sarah.

"It's either your net, Sarah," said Tim, "or bats

in your belfry." He waggled the net, bat and all, at Sarah's head. Sarah ducked, suppressing a scream.

Tink sat down in front of Tim, tongue lolling and tail wagging proudly, almost as if he'd caught the bat himself.

Jenny came out from behind Sarah. "That was fun. Do it again, Timmy, do it again!"

"Delighted," said Tim, and opened the closet door.

He expected a flurry of bat wings, and a quick battle—heroics on his part while the dog barked and the girls shrieked, but nothing happened. "Where are they?" he asked.

"In the back." Sarah wrenched the net from his hands and walked into the closet. With the handle of the net, she poked at something Tim had mistaken for a scarf.

"Ooooh!" squealed Jenny. "Look! Lots of 'em!"

Sarah's face was scrunched up, as if she were about to swallow something nasty. She took a big breath and prodded three bats toward Tim. When they swooped, he couldn't keep himself from ducking.

"See?" she said. "They do so go for your hair."

"Yeah, okay." Tim tried to grab the net from her, but she held on.

"I'll do it," she said grimly, opening the net— whereupon the first bat darted out and joined its fellows. Tink snapped at it but missed.

19

Jenny somehow had the presence of mind to close the door. "Now they have to stay here," she said smugly, sitting on her bed and looking for all the world as if she were at the movies.

"About that cardboard box," said Tim.

"Right. I'll get one." Sarah opened the door and slid out quickly, between bats.

"Get one with a lid," Tim called after her, and then he sat down next to Jenny to watch the show.

It was kind of disappointing, though. After a few half-hearted swoops and dog snaps, the bats settled down, two on the curtain rod, one under the desk-table, one under Sarah's bedside lamp, and one suspended from the empty top shelf of a bookcase. Tink sat in the middle of the room, barking unenthusiastically every so often. But finally he gave up and lay down quietly.

"They're sleeping," observed Jenny.

"I think you're right, Jen," Tim told her. "Bats sleep during the day."

"But these flew."

"We woke them up."

"Oh."

There was a knock at the door.

"It's safe," Tim called, and Sarah reentered, lugging boxes. "I got two," she said. "Both have lids."

"Great." Tim picked up the net. "How're we going to do this?"

Sarah was all business now. "I guess one of us

could do the catching and dumping into the box, and the other could keep the box closed between bats."

"What if the bat in the box flies out when we open it?"

"I don't know. Maybe it won't."

"Okay," said Tim. "I'll catch."

"No," said Sarah. "I'll catch."

Tim started to protest, but Sarah cut him off with "It's my net."

So Tim held the box open while Sarah snuck up on the two bats hanging from the curtain rod. With a deft swoop and twist, she managed to get both of them inside the net and drop them in the box. Tim slammed the cover shut and said sincerely, "Nice going!" Jenny clapped and Tink wagged his tail.

"Yes," said Sarah, "but the others won't be so easy. I'll have to get them one at a time. Let's start on the next box, though, so these don't get out."

"Okay."

The bat on the bookcase was next. It squeaked, but was otherwise cooperative.

"Now comes the hard part," Sarah said. "Which box should we open for the next bat?"

Tim put his ear first to one box, then to the other. "The one you just caught—What is it, Jenny?"

Jenny was tugging on Tim's sleeve. "I need a drink of water," she said. "Can I go?"

"No," said Sarah. "Not till we've gotten all the bats."

21

"But I'm thirsty," Jenny whined. "And it's no fun anymore."

"Jenny, sit down on your bed and *don't move*," commanded Sarah.

Jenny, visibly cowed, obeyed.

"Okay," said Tim. "Go for it, Sar'."

Like a hunter stalking big game in Africa, Sarah crept up on the bat under the desk. But it darted away before she was able to catch it, and flew up to the light fixture in the center of the ceiling.

"Great," said Tim. "Be careful you don't smash the light," he added as Sarah raised her net.

"I'm tryyyyy-ing!"

The bat flew to the curtain rod.

"This one's too lively," she said. "He'd get out of the box in a minute anyway, when we put his friend in. Let's get the other one and leave this one for last."

"Okay," Tim agreed. But just as Sarah dislodged the bat on the bedside lamp, poking it gently with the net and then trying to flip it in, Jenny opened the bedroom door, saying, "Tink's thirsty, too"— and both bats flew out.

"Oh, no!" exclaimed Tim.

"JENNY!" Sarah screeched. "I told you to stay still. Now see what you've done!"

Jenny burst into tears.

And the bats flew merrily around the hall, with Tink in gleeful pursuit.

chapter 4

Mr. B

It took Sarah and Tim another hour to calm Jenny down and catch the remaining bats. They put them in a third box, not wanting to risk opening the first two. Then they took the boxes outside into the woods, opened the lids, and ran. "We can get them tomorrow," Sarah said.

"What, the bats?" Tim asked mock innocently.

"No, you dope, the boxes."

"It's a good thing," Tim said, chuckling, "that Aunt Clara isn't here."

"Oh, wow," Sarah said. "Aunt Clara." She drew herself up to her full height. "Children," she declaimed in Aunt Clara's voice or something very like it, carefully stressing each syllable, "the bat is ac-tu-ally a most in-ter-es-ting animal. It lives most

of its life upside down, and is largely noc-tur-
nal."

Tim couldn't help laughing.

The next crisis was dinner. Neither Tim nor Sarah
had thought about it, so when they got back to the
cabin and Jenny whined, "I'm hungry," they looked
at each other in horror.

"We're going to have to cook," said Sarah, going
into the kitchen.

"*You're* going to have to cook," Tim said cheerfully. "That's the girl's job."

"Since when? Daddy cooks. Look at all the famous men chefs, too. We'll take turns cooking. And
planning meals. And shopping."

"What," asked Tim, "are we going to do about
money?"

Sarah looked at him blankly. "There's always our
allowances," she said after a terrible silence. "How
much do you have?"

"Maybe thirty dollars saved up."

"And I've got about the same. That should be
okay, if we're careful. Mom brought lots of stuff.
Maybe we'll only have to get milk and bread, that
kind of thing."

"Salad," said Tim. "Vegetables."

Sarah made a face. "Maybe," she said, "we won't
have to eat those. And maybe the Gibsons will invite us to dinner."

"They'll have to invite Jenny, too. Ordinarily, they wouldn't. Sarah, what are we going to say to the Gibsons?"

"I don't know." Sarah peered into the kitchen cabinets. "The truth, maybe. Look, here's spaghetti, and a jar of sauce. That ought to be easy."

"You have to cook spaghetti," Tim pointed out. "Do you know how?"

"Look on the box, dope," said Sarah.

"Pa-sketti," sang Jenny, coming in and dancing around them. "Pa-sketti, pa-sketti!"

" 'Bring four quarts of water to a boil,' " Tim read aloud. " 'Add spaghetti. Boil eight to twelve minutes.' That doesn't sound too hard."

He reached for a pot just as Jenny tugged at his sleeve and said, "Pasketti for supper. Pasketti for supper."

"We're making it," said Sarah. "Go play with Tink."

"Tink!" exclaimed Tim. "He needs supper, too." He located a can of dog food, tossed it to Sarah, and then looked in the refrigerator. "Mom brought lettuce," he said, "and tomatoes. I'm going to make a salad. Spaghetti's good for carbos, but Coach says to eat green stuff, too. I'm in training."

Sarah rolled her eyes. "Believe me, I know. Okay, I'll do the spaghetti. You do the salad. How much water is four quarts?"

The spaghetti tasted good, but it formed itself into logs while it was cooking, so instead of nice long floppy strings, the Hoskinses were faced with hard bars that needed to be cut. A lot of the sauce had boiled away, and there didn't seem to be any grated cheese or salad dressing. Tim tried to make dressing from oil and vinegar the way he'd seen his father do, but he didn't know how much of each to put in or what else to add, so it tasted kind of strange.

"What's for dessert?" Tim asked when they were through.

"Ice cream!" shouted Jenny. "Please?"

Tim looked at Sarah.

"There isn't any," she said. "But we could walk to the village and get some."

"It's over a mile, Sarah."

"So what?"

"That's too far for Jenny."

"You go then; you're the runner. I know—go on your bike, and bring back a half gallon."

"That costs money."

"We have to have dessert, Tim. Ice cream's easiest. Meanwhile, Jenny and I will get ready for bed, won't we, Jenny, and I'll read a story."

"Oh, goody," Jenny said. "I want *Pooh*."

"You got it," said Sarah. "Go on, Tim, scram."

"Whose allowance?" Tim asked.

"Doesn't matter." Sarah reached for a pad of pa-

per. "Here," she said. "We'll keep a record, okay?"
She wrote:

MONEY RECORD
Tim: $ _____ for ice cream

and held it up. "Okay?"

Tim sighed, figuring it would be useless to suggest that they start with Sarah's allowance instead. He went outside, whistling to Tink, who unfolded himself from the front step and pranced off happily behind the bike.

It was a nice evening, coolish, with the sun's afterglow making a gleaming line along the bay and decorating the tops of the spruce trees with gold. Tim felt good as he pedaled up to the main road.

Tomorrow, he thought, I'll really start training: run in the morning, then go to Blue Loon Lake for a swim in the midafternoon. He decided to save his toughening-up cold-water swims for when John could follow him in the dinghy . . .

Suddenly he was surprised to meet a pocket of fog so thick he had to turn on his bike light.

"Good evening."

Tim turned, so startled he wobbled a little; he hadn't heard anyone behind him. But Tink was barking, and there was someone there: a pale, dark-haired young man on a fancier bike than Tim's, a thirteen-speed, maybe. The man was dressed in black biking shorts, gloves, and a black helmet with a red stripe on it. His T-shirt was also black with a red stripe, and he was very thin and solemn-looking—not winded at all, either, though he must have been pedaling pretty fast.

"Hi," Tim said as the man pulled up beside him. "Foggy night, isn't it? Shut up, Tink!" Tink wasn't just barking anymore; he was beginning to growl, which was very unlike him.

"Indeed it is," said the man, in a slight accent Tim couldn't place. He gave Tink a wary glance. "You are handling that bicycle very well. I was watching you as I was riding along."

"Thanks," said Tim. "I'm training for a race, actually. Well, not right now; right now I'm getting ice cream for my sisters, but most of the time, I'm training."

"Oh?" The man raised his eyebrows, which Tim saw were thick and so long they met above his nose. "What is the race, if I may be asking?"

Tim, holding Tink, who was curling his lips back and actually snarling, told the man about the Iron Boy Triathlon and his coach and his training program. He ended by saying, "I kind of miss my coach, though; it's better if you've got someone watching you. You know, your form and stuff. If I slip, I might not even know."

The man raised his eyebrows again, and his thin nose flared a little. "I could perhaps be obliging you there," he said. "In fact, I would be enjoying that very much. I am a bit of a racer myself. And I—er—how is it?—I am participating in all of your three sports. The running is perhaps my best, but I am not bad at the swimming or the cycling. I have"—here he ducked his head modestly—"won a few trophies long ago."

"That's great," Tim said, impressed. "Sure, I— It'd be great if you'd help, Mr.—er . . ."

"Biancu. But you may be calling me Mr. B. It is easier, no?"

"Yes," said Tim gratefully, thinking the foreign name must account for the accent. "Thank you. Tinkerfield, shut up!" He gave Tink's collar a little jerk. It's a good thing, he thought, that no dog show judges can see him now.

"So," said Mr. B, eyeing Tink nervously, "tomorrow at the same time and place, yes? Perhaps without our friend here?" He nodded toward Tink, who bared his teeth rudely.

"Definitely without our friend," agreed Tim, embarrassed and annoyed. He hesitated, then added, "But I usually train during the day."

"Ah," said Mr. B. "But during the day, I have— er—I am working at a job. So it must be night, eh? You can be doing your usual training in the day; then you can be showing me in the night what you have done or what you are wanting to—er—perfect, yes?"

"Okay," said Tim; that sounded reasonable enough. "Thanks."

"It is my pleasure," Mr. B said with a courtly little bow, and pedaled off.

It wasn't until later, after he'd bought the ice cream and was hurrying to get home before it melted, that Tim wondered how on earth Mr. B was going to be able to coach him in the dark.

chapter 5

Famous Last Words

Sarah and Jenny were waiting on the porch in their nightgowns when Tim arrived, carrying the ice cream.

"More bat mices!" Jenny squealed when he and Tink joined them. "Lots more."

Tim looked inquiringly at Sarah.

"It's true," she said in a choked voice. "All over." She held out her hand for the ice cream, and Tim realized she was close to tears, which was unusual for Sarah. He also saw that she'd set out plates and spoons on the porch table, as if she didn't want to go back inside, and that there was a pile of sleeping bags in the corner. Tink, who had calmed down as soon as Mr. B had left, curled up on them with a contented sigh.

"What happened?" Tim asked tentatively as Sarah began to dish out the dessert.

"We got undressed," she said, her voice barely under control. "And I started reading *Pooh*. And then they came back, a huge bunch of them."

"Hun'reds!" exclaimed Jenny enthusiastically. "Hun'reds and hun'reds!"

"Well, maybe not hundreds, Jen," said Sarah, "but"—she handed Tim a brimming bowl—"but lots, more than before. They kept swooping around . . ."

"And Sarah screamed again." Jenny took her bowl from Sarah and sat down cross-legged on the bench at the porch table.

"I did not, Jenny."

"You did so. But *I* didn't." Jenny nodded emphatically. "I like bat mices."

"Sarah." Tim put a brotherly hand on her shoulder. "How many really?"

Sarah shook her head. "I don't know. Ten. Fifteen. All over the place."

Tim picked up the serving spoon, which Sarah had put down, and held up the ice cream carton questioningly. Sarah shook her head, and Tim knew then just how upset she was; ordinarily, she never refused ice cream. He put back some of the ice cream she'd given him—too much fat and sugar, he knew Coach would say—and reached out to open the door to the Big Room.

"No!" Sarah shrieked. "Don't go in there!"

"Sarah, the ice cream will melt if I don't put it away. And maybe the bats will come out if I open the door. Wouldn't that be a good idea?"

"Yes, but I opened the windows in the Big Room, screens and all. And the bats didn't budge."

"Well, maybe now they will."

"I'm not going back in there, Tim. I'm sleeping on the porch."

"*I'm* not sleeping on the porch unless I have to," Tim said firmly, and he opened the door.

There was no sign of the bats. He walked cautiously across the Big Room into the kitchen. One small bat was suspended from the kitchen faucet, so Tim carefully opened the window and screen above the sink and then poked the bat, gently guiding it out. He put the ice cream away, closed the screen and the screens in the Big Room, and headed for the stairs.

There were two bats under the spiral. Gingerly, he wrapped first one and then the other in dishtowels and shook the towels out the kitchen door.

Upstairs seemed clear, so he called the girls in.

"One bat," warned Sarah, "and I'm going back outside."

"The bats," Tim said patiently, "are outside. You'll be safer in here. They'll probably stay out now, Sarah. And if we keep the screens down and are careful of doors, they won't be able to get back in."

"Hah!" Sarah took Jenny's hand and headed for

33

her room, while Tim and Tink went into theirs. "I hope that's not famous last words."

It *was* famous last words. At dawn, the sun woke Tim. He staggered sleepily into the bathroom only to see something small and limp and black hanging from the showerhead. Good thing, he thought, pulling on his running shorts, that I shower *after* I run.

But when he got back from running, not only was the bat still there, but the door to the girls' room was open and Sarah was sitting up in bed, wide-eyed, staring out her window.

"What's up?" Tim asked, peering in at her, whispering because Jenny was still asleep in the other bed.

"Bats," Sarah whispered back. "Hundreds of them—really. Flying through the sky just as it got light. I couldn't even yell."

"Maybe you dreamed it." Tim looked out her window. "Couldn't you have?"

"I could have," Sarah said angrily, "but I didn't. They were heading right for the house."

"Well, they're not *in* the house, Sarah, are they?" Tim said, angry himself now. The run had been wonderful; he'd gone along the beach on a path he knew above the rocks, and had then turned inland and run along a marsh where red-winged black-birds dipped and soared and gulls wheeled overhead. He'd enjoyed the air and the morning and the sky and the warming sun, but best of all, he'd put in a really fast time and he wanted to think about that, not about bats.

But Sarah was out of bed, and her hand was on her closet door. "I just bet . . ." she said grimly—and wrenched the door open.

Tim whistled in spite of himself. There, neatly hanging along the closet pole, was a row of small black bats, wings folded, eyes shut, unmoving, sleeping . . .

"Exterminator!" Sarah ran out of the room and down the spiral.

Tim closed the closet door and followed her. "It's only seven-thirty," he reminded her as she flipped through the yellow pages. "Better wait till nine. Did you actually see them come into your room?"

"No." Sarah had stopped flipping pages. "There are only three exterminators here."

"That's better than none," Tim remarked vaguely, still focused on the bats themselves. "Where were they heading?"

Sarah looked puzzled. "The exterminators?"

"No, stupid, the bats."

"I don't know. Sort of for the roof, I guess."

"The thing is, how did they get into your closet? Was your screen open?"

"What, do you think I'm crazy or something?"

Tim didn't honor that with a reply. There's got

to be a way in through Sarah's closet from the outside, he thought. He bounded up the spiral again,
bumping into Tink who was on his way down,
rushed into Sarah's room, and yanked the closet
door open. Trying to ignore the sleeping bats, he
pushed the clothes aside—and there, way in the
back, was a hole. Not a very big hole, but a hole
nonetheless.

"Sarah," he yelled. "I think I've found it!"

Right after breakfast, they plugged the hole with
rags and cardboard. Then they got Jenny and Tink
started on a game of stick outside, and when that
was well under way, they went into their parents'
room, opened the trapdoor in the ceiling, and let
down the folding ladder that led to the attic.

"Oh, my!" exclaimed Tim, who was first up the
ladder. He stopped so abruptly that Sarah crashed
into him.

"What?" she asked.

"Maybe you don't want to see."

"Oh, come on, Tim, I'm getting used to it. It's
just when they surprise me and swoop around that
I hate them." She peered around him. "How
bad—"

She stopped, and they both stood there trans-
fixed. Hanging from the rafters was a whole colony
of bats, at least thirty or forty: big ones, small ones,

in-between ones. A few were brownish in color, but most of them were black.

There was bat guano on the floor, and a funny smell.

"Take me out, coach," whispered Tim.

"Exterminator," whispered Sarah.

"Yes," Tim answered, and they backed down the ladder as quickly as they could, folded it up into the ceiling again, closed the trapdoor tightly, and went straight to the phone.

But that didn't work either.

ABC EXTERMINATORS didn't do bats.

BUG OFF EXTERMINATORS was strictly an insect operation.

FOSDICK AND FOSTER SURE SHOT EX-TERMINATORS did bats, but their bat man was on vacation and wouldn't be back till after the Fourth of July.

"We can't wait that long," said Sarah, sinking down on the sofa. "What are we going to do?"

"Ask the Gibsons?"

"We can't ask them," Sarah replied. "They'll know we're alone if we do."

"Maybe the postmistress. We could say we're asking for Mom and Dad."

Sarah shook her head. "Suppose she decides to call Mom and Dad up and give advice over the phone?"

"We could always say Mom and Dad are out."

"It's too risky."

"How about the hardware store guy then?" asked Tim. "He never remembers who we are."

Sarah brightened a little. "Maybe. But—"

The phone rang.

"Blast," said Tim. He reached for it. "Hello?"

"Tim, darling, good morning."

Tim's heart sank. "It's Mom," he mouthed to Sarah, who rolled her eyes and mouthed back, "Don't tell."

"How was your first night?" Mom asked. "Are you all okay?"

"Oh, fine," Tim said heartily. "Just terrific."

"Did Aunt Clara get there all right?"

"Oh, yeah. Yeah, she did. She—ah—she's taking a shower."

"Oh? I thought she usually took baths—at night."

"Well, yeah, I guess it's a bath," Tim said hastily. "She—she was too tired last night."

"Oh. Well, give her my love when she comes out. What did you have for dinner?"

"Dinner? Spa—"

"Roast beef," Sarah mouthed, waggling his arm.

"Er—roast beef," Tim said into the phone.

"Lovely," Mom replied. "Aunt Clara does that so well! And you'll have plenty left over for sandwiches, won't you? And maybe another meal as well."

"Oh, yes," said Tim brightly. "Sandwiches."

"Are you all right, dear? You sound a little odd."

"I—I just came in from a run. You know how that is. I feel a little funny sometimes afterwards. I did a really fast time today. Want to speak to Sarah?"

Sarah shook her head violently.

"Sure," said Mom. "You be good, dear. I love you. Dad sends his love, too."

"I love you, too, Mom." Relieved that he hadn't made a really bad slip, Tim handed the phone to Sarah, and then remembered what he really wanted to ask—but Sarah asked it for him.

"How's Grandpa?" he heard her say. "Oh, good. . . . Yes, Jenny's fine. . . . So's Tink. Mom, everything's really okay. . . . Yes, I will. . . . I love you, too. Love to Daddy and Granny and Grandpa. . . . Yes, I will. . . . Bye." When Sarah hung up, her face was decidedly red and there was sweat beading on her brow.

"How's Grandpa?" Tim asked.

"About the same. No worse, at least. That was awful."

"Yeah. But we did okay."

Tink barked outside and they heard Jenny's voice saying, "Hi," and a moment later John Gibson strode into the cabin, bearing a large box of strawberries. "From Mom," he said, and put the box down with a Gibson the Great bow and flourish. "Plus a din-

ner invite for tonight after my magic show. I told
Mom we were taking Jenny to the show and asked
if she could come to dinner, too. She said fine.
And Dad says we can have the dinghy Saturday.
Hi, Sarah!"

"Good man," said Tim, taking the strawberries.

"Hi, John," said Sarah. "Do you know an exterminator?"

chapter 6

Gibson the Great

John didn't.

There was plenty of time before the magic show, which was at a children's birthday party in the late afternoon, so Tim, Sarah, and John walked to the village with Tink and Jenny tagging along. They'd decided to go swimming later, so Tim could get his practice in.

In the village they stopped at the post office to see if the Hoskinses had any mail yet, for almost no one in Starfish Harbor had mail delivered to their houses.

Mrs. Loring, the postmistress, exclaimed happily when they walked in. "Welcome!" she said, her plump face beaming. "When did you folks blow in?"

"Night before last," said Sarah.

"How are all of you? Why, Jenny," she said, leaning over the counter and not giving them time to answer, "you've grown at least a foot! Now let's just see. Come right around here in the back."

Jenny giggled and went behind the counter to the four-foot ruler taped to the wall, where Mrs. Loring measured all the town's children until they were old enough to be in school. She'd added the Hoskins kids when Sarah was three, right along with the town kids, and that, the Gibsons had told the Hoskinses, meant they were almost natives.

"Well," said Mrs. Loring, coming out again with Jenny, "not quite a foot, but a good two inches since last September! No, dear, no mail yet," she said to Tim, "unless you count the seed catalog your mother always gives to old Mrs. Perkins each year because you get another copy back in Boston."

"Please give it to Mrs. Perkins again," Sarah said primly.

"Why, thank you, dear, I will. How *is* your mother? And your dad? He was looking a mite peaked in April when you were all here for Easter."

"He's okay," said Tim. "He's a little worried about—" Sarah came down hard on his foot—and just in time too, for he'd been about to say "worried about our grandfather." He quickly changed it to "worried about his job," and Mrs. Loring clucked sympathetically and said, "My word, yes! I'm not surprised, what with the state of things these days. Your dad's in computers, isn't he?"

"That's right," replied Sarah politely. "But now he thinks his job is pretty safe."

"That's a blessing. Jobs around here, goodness knows, are scarce as hens' teeth."

"Speaking of jobs," John said innocently, "do you know any exterminators? Anyone who does bats, I mean?"

There was a brief horrified silence from the older Hoskinses. Then Jenny piped up: "We've got—ow, Sarah!" she squealed, and Tim knew Sarah had come down on Jenny's foot, too.

He scowled at John, but John said, in his most charming I-know-how-to-deal-with-adults voice, "Yes, I've got this pen pal out in Ohio. There's an old barn on his dad's farm and it's just full of bats. They can't find an exterminator to clear it out. I wondered if anyone in town might have any tips I could give him."

"Let me see," said Mrs. Loring. "It's been a bad year for bats around here, too, but most folks just take care of them on their own. Jeff Willard might be about your best bet. I could ask him; he had quite a few down to his place, I think. Now, speaking of that boy in Ohio," she went on, "you got something from him today. And your folks have some bills and a postcard." She reached behind the counter while John gave Sarah and Tim a broad wink.

"I was afraid you didn't have a pen pal in Ohio," said Tim when they were safely outside again, "and that she'd know because she's postmistress and everything."

"I'm not that dumb." John stuffed his family's mail into his back pocket. "Harry Cates."

"Huh?" said Sarah, taking Jenny's hand as they crossed the street to the town dock.

"Harry Cates. That's the guy in Ohio I write to. And he does live on a farm, and he did say there are sometimes bats in his dad's barn. If there's one thing you learn in magic," John went on as they walked out on the dock, "it's to stick as close to reality as possible. The other thing you learn," he added, making an airy gesture above Jenny's head and then pointing out to sea—they all followed his pointing hand—"is to distract people from what you're really doing. PRESTO!" He pulled a plastic rose out of Jenny's hair and presented it to her with an elegant bow. "Just practicing," he said.

They walked to the end of the dock and back again, inspecting the boats tied up on both sides of it. Afterwards they went into the hardware store, where John bought some nails for his dad; they decided not to ask about bats there after all. Then they stopped at the grocer's for a loaf of bread and at the drugstore for toothpaste and a newspaper, all for Mrs. Gibson. Everywhere they went people said "Welcome back!" or "How was your winter?" or "Good to see you again!" to Tim, Sarah, and Jenny, and by the time they headed home for lunch, Tim felt the warm glow that coming back to Starfish Harbor always gave him and going back to Boston never did.

They stopped at the Gibsons' to deliver the mail, the bread, the nails, the paper, and the toothpaste. Then they walked through the woods to the Hoskinses', and while Tink, Jenny, and John ran down to the beach, Sarah and Tim went to the cabin to make sandwiches for lunch.

Stuck in the kitchen door was a small white card:

VORTESCU EXTERMINATORS
Specializing in Bats
Summer cottages, barns, stables, etc.
NO JOB TOO SMALL!
555-9872

"Great!" said Tim.

Sarah frowned. "How did they know we were looking?"

"Well, we did call those other places," Tim reminded her. "Maybe ABC or Bug Off or Fosdick and Foster told them. Not everyone advertises in the yellow pages. Besides, people always go around neighborhoods with business cards and things like that. Remember? We get them at home all the time. Carpet cleaning, taxi service, that kind of thing."

"This isn't," said Sarah, "that kind of thing."

Tim shrugged and reached for the phone. "Don't look a gift bat specialist in the mouth."

"Ha ha," Sarah said unenthusiastically.

Tim dialed, and after two rings, a voice said, "You have reached 555-9872, Vortescu Exterminators. We cannot be coming to the telephone right now, but if you leave a message, we will be getting back to you this evening. Thank you for calling. No job too small, no bats too large."

"Cute," muttered Tim, and when the beep came, he said, "This is Timothy Hoskins on Cape Point Road, left fork and first driveway to the left. We have a—um—bat problem. Number is 555-9435. Thank you."

"I don't like this," Sarah said darkly, slamming a can of tuna fish down on the kitchen counter. "I don't like it at all."

"Oh, come on, Sar'. It's just a coincidence."

"We'll see." She wrenched the lid off the mayonnaise jar as if it were a bat's neck. "You know what Mom says about coincidences."

"No," said Tim, pausing, his hand on the breadbox. "What does Mom say about coincidences?"

Sarah giggled. "I don't remember. But she said

something about them once, and it wasn't good. Bread, please."

The beach picnic they decided to have was only moderately gritty; the beach in front of the cabin was more rock than sand, so it was better than most beaches for meals. And the rocks were good for climbing on, which they did for a while after finishing their sandwiches. After that, John went home to get ready for his show, and Sarah, Tim, Jenny, and Tink set out for Blue Loon Lake for a swim.

It was a longish walk, but when they got there, and Tim slipped into the water and swam far out, leaving the others paddling close to shore, he felt all his worries about bats and exterminators and Grandpa and Aunt Clara slipping away. The water was pretty cold, but not as cold as the ocean would be, and he warmed up quickly in it. For a while he just swam, letting his muscles loosen and his mind relax, and then he started his underwater watch and struck out for the opposite shore, which looked about a quarter of a mile away. He had to turn before he reached it, for the water got too shallow to go on swimming, but that was all right. He checked his watch as he turned, and saw that his time was pretty good, although not great. But swimming wasn't his strong point anyway, and his coach had suggested that he just try to hold his own and concentrate on running and his best event, biking. He wanted to try to improve his swimming some, though; it wouldn't do to risk floundering or getting worn out in his first event . . .

He felt the water tugging at his legs, his arms—he felt leaden, exhausted—but he knew he had to go on; he couldn't give up—and there was the bike race and the run to go . . .

"Tim, Tim!"

It was Sarah, waving her arms on the shore. He'd lost track of time, as usual. "What?" he shouted back, treading water.

"We've got to get going. John's on at that party at four."

"What time is it now?"

"Quarter past three."

Reluctantly, Tim swam to shore.

The party was near the cabin, but John's show was already under way by the time they arrived.

Little kids were sitting in rows on the floor of a big, airy living room. The hostess showed Jenny to a spot in the front and invited Sarah and Tim to sit on chairs in the back with the grownups. John, in a flowing red satin cape with a tall pointy hat to match, stood next to a table draped with a white cloth. He had a false mustache pasted on his upper lip. "And now," he was saying in a deep un-John-like voice as he waved a long stick coated with spangles, "observe, ladies and gentlemen." He put down the spangly stick-wand and picked up a piece of newspaper. "One ordinary newspaper, right? The kind you read every day—or your parents do, right?"

"Right!" shouted the little kids.

John rolled the piece of newspaper into a tube shape. Then he rolled another—and another—and another, saying things like "Here's one more" and "This one wants to play, too" each time, till he had about six pieces of newspaper in one big tube. Finally, as Tim moved a little so he could watch more closely, John squashed his giant tube and made some rips in the top of it, talking all the time and flapping the ripped edges down so they hung around the top of the tube like petals.

"So?" Sarah whispered, rolling her eyes at Tim. "Big deal, huh?"

But then there was a gasp from the audience, and Tim heard even Sarah join in as John pulled up from inside the tube—and up and up and up—until he had a huge tower of newspaper reaching well above his head, with "petals" hanging down from each section.

"The Tree of Life," John announced triumphantly, bowing.

From then on Tim's eyes were riveted on his friend, and he knew that Sarah's were, too. John

49

made a nickel disappear and reappear under a paper cone, fashioned a rabbit out of a plain white handkerchief and made it jump along his arm when kids from the audience patted it, broke a toothpick and made it whole again. For his grand finale, while the whole audience held its breath, John cut the hostess's teenage son in half with a rope. Then he put him together again, and everyone cheered.

"Of course I didn't really cut him in half," John admitted when it was over and they were walking back to the Gibsons' for dinner. "It's just an illusion."

"Yes, you did too do it," Jenny insisted, holding John's hand as they walked and looking up at him admiringly. "You did and it was real magic!"

"Ha!" Sarah snorted. When Jenny finally ran off to pick some flowers for Mrs. Gibson, she said to John, "Okay, how did you do it?"

"That would be telling," John said with a mysterious smile. "And Gibson the Great never tells."

chapter 7

"No Job Too Small"

Tim had never been very fond of grownups, aside from his own family, his coach, and a couple of teachers, but the Gibsons were an exception. Mr. Gibson was big and blustery, the way Tim pretty much figured most lobstermen were, with a face red from sun and wind and salt spray, and hands raw from hauling lobster traps. But his eyes were kind, and he never failed to make people feel welcome in his house or on his boat. Mrs. Gibson, a stout, comfortable woman, always seemed to know when you needed a smile or a snack, and gave you either without hesitation.

But this evening Mr. Gibson was subdued and Mrs. Gibson looked worried, though both of them greeted the Hoskinses warmly and hugged them when they arrived.

"It's Emily," John said when they were washing up and Tim asked him why his parents were so quiet. "They're worried about her. You'll see." He paused, drying his hands. "Funny," he commented. "The lady who gave that party? She said one of the little kids she'd invited couldn't come because he's sick. Listless, she said, and won't eat and hardly ever wants to play. He's been having bad dreams, she said, too. I heard her telling one of the other mothers."

"Why is that funny?" Tim asked.

"Sounds just like Emily," John said. "Like I said, you'll see."

And indeed, the change in Emily was startling. She floated into the dining room after they were all sitting down; Mrs. Gibson had called her twice before she came. She'd always moved gracefully, like a dancer, but this was different; she walked as if she weren't on the ground at all, but skimming over it, a few inches up. Her face was very pale, and she looked as if she'd lost about ten pounds— which made her painfully thin.

"Hi, Em," Sarah said heartily after a worried glance at Tim. She jumped up and gave Emily a hug.

Tim blinked; he knew he'd been staring, but he

couldn't stop. He could see that Jenny was staring, too.

"Hello," Emily said languidly. She didn't hug Sarah back, Tim noticed, just let her arms hang by her sides, as if she didn't have the strength to lift them.

It was like that all through the meal. Emily hardly spoke, though Sarah asked her several times about what she'd done since they'd last seen her. She hardly ate either, and she asked to be excused before dessert.

"All right, dear," said Mrs. Gibson. "But why don't you and Sarah take your desserts to your room so you can have a nice talk?"

"Oh, Mom," Emily said, sounding almost the way Jenny did when she was whining. "I'm so sleepy. I'm sorry, Sarah. It's really good to see you. Maybe tomorrow, okay?"

"Sure, Em," Sarah answered with a smile Tim knew was forced. "I'll come over in the morning."

"Well . . ." Emily began, but Mrs. Gibson interrupted. "That would be wonderful, Sarah," she said. "Emily would love it. Wouldn't you, dear?"

"Yes, Mom," Emily said meekly. She smiled wanly at Sarah. "Good night," she said. "Pleasant dreams."

"What a weird thing to say," Sarah commented as she, Tim, and Jenny walked home, carrying a

borrowed flashlight. It was just about time, Tim
realized, when he saw how dark it was, to meet
Mr. B; he didn't want to keep him waiting.

"What was weird?" he asked absently.

"The way Emily said 'Pleasant dreams.' As if we
were all going right to bed."

"Well," said Tim, "*she* was going to bed, wasn't
she? I mean, she said she was sleepy, and . . .
What's this?"

They had just turned into the driveway, and Tink,
whom they'd left at home, was barking furiously at
a small white van that had just pulled up in front
of the cabin. "VORTESCU EXTERMINATORS,"
it said on the side. "No Job Too Small!"

"That was quick," Tim said cheerfully. "Tink,
NO!" he shouted, and ran toward the van. He could
see two men inside, obviously afraid to get out with
the dog barking so vigorously.

"Oh, my goodness," said one of the men, gray-
haired, thin, and ghostly pale. "Oh, my gracious. I
do thank you so much, sir. That dog is vicious!"
He climbed out of the van, eyeing Tink nervously.

"He's not really vicious," said Tim, irritated at
that but flattered at being called sir. "He's just not
used to strangers. Cool it, Tink!"

But Tim knew it wasn't true about Tink and
strangers; Tink had always been super friendly. He
frowned, remembering how Tink had acted with
Mr. B, too. It just wasn't like him at all.

The other man got out of the van as Sarah came up with Jenny. He was taller than the first, and seemed to be quite a bit younger, but his face was hidden under a wide-brimmed black hat—to keep bats from swooping at him, Tim guessed. "Good evening," the younger man said, bowing formally, his voice muffled by the flowing ascot he wore around his neck and way up over his chin—but he sounded oddly familiar even so. "We are Vortescu Exterminators." He nodded toward the older man. "This is my partner, Mr. Vortescu. You are requiring our assistance, yes? We have come as soon as we have been able. Where are the bats, please?"

Jenny giggled and pointed at the floppy hat.

"Shh, Jen," said Sarah softly. "That's not polite. They're in the house," she went on in her normal voice after glancing at Tim. "But I really think it'd be better . . ."

Tim pulled her aside. "Better if what?" he whispered.

"If we wait," she whispered back. "They're so weird, Tim."

"Anyone," said Tim, "who specializes in getting rid of bats is bound to be weird." He looked at his watch. "Look, the trouble is that I've got to go meet that guy."

"Tim, I really wish . . ." Sarah began, and Jenny whined, "I'm scared"—but Tim knew he had no

way of communicating with Mr. B, and he didn't
want to lose out on having a private coach.

"We either tell the exterminators to go away,"
he said to Sarah, "and keep the bats for at least
another night, or we let them in now. And I've got
to go meet Mr. B. Come on, Sar', I know you can
do it!"

Sarah sighed. "Okay, but I don't like it."

"I owe you one," Tim said. He turned back to
the men, who were unloading an impressive array
of tanks, hoses, and cans from their van. "I have to
go," he told them, "but my sister will show you
the bats." Under his breath he said to Sarah, "Just
tell them where they are if you're nervous. Stay
outside, and keep Tink and Jenny outside, too, while
they're working. They probably spray poison or
something."

"You couldn't pay me to be in the house with
those two," said Sarah, "or to let Jenny in. Look at
Tink. I wish you'd stay."

Tink, who had backed away a bit, was growling
softly, and the hair on the back of his neck was
standing up. Sarah took him by the collar and he
strained against it, still growling.

Maybe I shouldn't go, thought Tim. He had to
admit there was something sort of odd about the
whole situation. But it wasn't as if this was the city,
where there were criminals and con men and other
dangers. This was just little Starfish Harbor, Maine,

where nothing much bad ever happened. And besides, the Gibsons were just a shout away through
the woods.

The older man had been watching them. "My
goodness," he said, "you need not be here while
we work. Oh, my goodness, no. Just show us where
the bats are, and we will take care of them, no
matter how many or how few." He gave them an
oily smile. " 'No job too small,' you know," he went
on, pointing to the slogan on the van. " 'No bats
too large.' It will not take us long. You have perhaps a neighbor you could go to for"—he reached
into his pocket and pulled out a huge, heavy gold
watch on an equally heavy chain—"twenty to thirty
minutes?"

"You could go back to the Gibsons'," said Tim to
Sarah. "You and Tink and Jenny. If you go by the
road, it'll take you a good ten minutes each way. If
you stay for another ten, they'll be done by the
time you get back. Here." He handed her the
flashlight they'd borrowed from the Gibsons. "Say
you're returning the flashlight. I'll just get a couple
more from the house, one for you to come back
with and one for me. I've got to go in for a minute," he told the exterminators.

"Then," said the younger, muffled man, "you can
be showing us where the bats are. After you." He
gestured Tim to the door. Tim held it open so the
men could bring in their equipment.

Tink kept a wary eye on them, pulling on Sarah's arm as she held him, and snarling and snapping as the men passed by.

"We're coming with you, Tim," Sarah said when Tim came out again with the flashlights. "Jenny's scared, and I can hardly hold Tink back. There's that old red wagon under the house in case Jenny gets tired."

Tim sighed. Maybe she was right. Jenny looked dangerously close to crying, and Tink was still growling softly and watching the cabin door and the van. What would Mom and Dad say if he left Sarah and Jenny and Tink there and something bad happened to them? For that matter, how would he feel? They could all wait while he trained with Mr. B. Maybe it would even be fun to have an audience. And Sarah could probably keep Tink from being too much of a pest.

"Okay," he said to Sarah. "But let's get going. I'm already late."

chapter 8

An Intruder?

The red wagon was under the house, and Jenny
calmed down as soon as Tim and Sarah told her she
was going to have a ride in it. But Mr. B wasn't
waiting for Tim at their meeting place, and he didn't
come, even though they waited nearly half an hour.

"Maybe he didn't mean it," Tim said disconso-
lately as they pulled Jenny home in the moonlight
with Tink, himself again, trotting beside them. "I
bet he didn't. A guy with trophies . . ."

"You don't need him, I bet," Sarah said kindly.
"After all, your school coach didn't say you needed
extra help or anything." They turned down the
driveway. "Tink!"

Tink had bolted ahead, growling once more, and
he actually dove at the wheels of the white van,

which was just pulling out. He nipped at them as Tim ran forward and grabbed him around the neck. "Bad dog!" Tim shouted. "You could've been run over!" He glanced apologetically up at the van, and the younger man, who was driving, nodded, his hat bobbing, and waved.

Then the man rolled down the window a little and, his face and accented voice still muffled, said, "We are finished. You will not be being troubled anymore with bats, I think."

"Thanks," said Tim. "Sorry about the dog."

The man shrugged.

"Will there be a funny smell?" Sarah called, stooping to the now sleeping Jenny and grasping her under the arms.

"A—I beg pardon?"

"A funny smell." Sarah walked over to the van. "You know, from the chemicals. When we had our apartment in Boston done for cockroaches, it smelled awful."

"Cockroaches?"

Tim looked hopefully beyond the driver to the passenger seat, thinking that perhaps the older man could explain to his partner about cockroaches. But he couldn't see the older man.

"Crawling insects," said Tim. "It doesn't matter. Can we call you again if we find more bats?"

"Of course. But there is being no more need, I think." Without any further conversation or even a goodbye, the man stepped down hard on the accelerator and sped off. Only then did Tink, who had been growling softly the whole time, relax.

"That's funny," Sarah said, frowning. "I didn't see his friend."

"Huh?" Tim was still puzzling over the younger man's voice. Then it hit him. Of course! It was the same as the voice on the answering machine. Relieved, he turned back to Sarah, who was saying in an annoyed way, "I said I didn't see his friend. The other guy."

"Neither did I," Tim admitted, shrugging it off. "But it's dark, Sarah. He must have been there."

Sarah pointed to the sky, where a nearly full moon hung over the spruce trees and made a silver path across the bay. "It's not that dark. I can see you clearly."

"Oh, well," Tim said, not wanting to admit he was uneasy, too. "Maybe he was bending down tying his shoe or something. Come on, I'll help you with Jenny. Let's go, Tink." Sarah and Tim made a chair of their hands and together managed to slide Jenny onto it, drape her arms around their necks, and carry her inside. Tink followed them willingly to the steps, and stuck his nose in the kitchen door behind them, but then he drew back, growling again, as if he was afraid to go inside.

"I've *had* it with you!" Tim said angrily, dragging him inside.

"Tim, that's mean," Sarah scolded. "Besides"—her eyes darted around the Big Room—"what if there's a robber or something?"

"Come on, Sarah, you're imagining things," he said as they eased Jenny down on the sofa. "How could there be when the exterminators were just here?" But he felt a thin stab of fear, nonetheless. They'd often joked that Tink would show a robber the TV set and the silver if one ever broke in. But he sure didn't look as if he'd do that now!

Tim went to the dog and knelt down, stroking his floppy ears. "Tink," he said, "what is it, boy?"

Tink wagged his tail, but he also whimpered, and his eyes kept darting to the stairs.

"Up there," Sarah whispered. "It's up there, whatever it is. Maybe we ought to call the police."

"It's probably just a leftover bat," Tim whispered back. "Or maybe Tink's sensitive to the chemical smell."

"There isn't," Sarah pointed out, "any chemical smell."

"Not to us." Tim got Tink's leash and snapped it onto his collar. "But maybe there is to a dog. Come on, Tinkerfield." Swallowing his fear, Tim led Tink to and then up the spiral.

Tink went readily enough into Tim's room, the girls' room, and the bathroom, but he balked every time they passed Mr. and Mrs. Hoskins's door.

Sarah, watching from the bottom of the spiral, said, "It's in Mom and Dad's room, Tim."

62

"I know," he said irritably. He cleared his throat, and, feeling more than a little silly, said in a loud voice, "COME OUT OF THERE, WHOEVER YOU ARE!"

"Or *what*ever you are," whispered Sarah, who had climbed partway up the stairs.

"Shut up, Sarah!" Tim snapped. "I don't need your weird horror stuff now."

"Sorry. I was just trying to cheer myself up." She came the rest of the way up the stairs and put a friendly hand on his arm. "Like you've said yourself a million times, that's all pretend. Make-believe. Hollywood."

"Look at Tink."

Sarah did, and backed away a step or two. "He's staring at the ceiling," she said softly. Then she laughed. "Well, of course he is!" She pointed up.

There, hanging from the edge of the trapdoor, one foot stuck in its crack, was a very small, very frightened-looking bat.

Sarah and Tim both laughed so loud they woke Jenny up.

He bent low against the wind, his hair still wet under his helmet, and his legs revolving faster and faster, toes clamped to the pedals. His muscles stretched now, warming in the sun; that water had been cold, *colder than anything he'd ever experienced. But now, biking along the straight road, he felt elated, optimistic; only five others were ahead, he knew, and he hadn't even gotten up to cruising speed . . .*

A tall, athletic-looking man rode up behind him. "I am sorry I was not meeting you," the man said; he was riding a coal-black bike and wearing black biking shorts and a tight-fitting black T-shirt, with a red stripe and a small capelike collar flowing over his back. "I had a pressing engagement, an emergency."

"Oh, that's all right," Tim heard himself say—and the man vanished and Tim was riding alone again, except his bike had become a sled and the road was snow-covered and icy. A sleigh burst out of the drifts ahead and sped toward him; it was drawn by six black horses, their nostrils flaring and their breath steaming in the now wintry air.

As they plunged past, Tim heard the crack of a whip and saw the coachman, a tall spare figure dressed in black, standing up, urging the horses on; their eyes were round and white with fear. The coach swirled by and Tim could just make out the man inside: short, thin, pale, with gray hair . . .

With a sharp laugh that startled him awake, Tim sat up in bed, rubbing his eyes. "Sheesh, what a dream!" he exclaimed, putting the pieces together: the missing Mr. B, the "No Job Too Small!" van,

the older exterminator—all transformed into something out of . . .

Tim stopped rubbing his eyes.

. . . out of one of Sarah's vampire stories, he
realized he'd been going to say. Out of *Dracula*, in
fact.

Shuddering, he swung his legs out of bed, high
to avoid bumping Tink—but then he was jolted fully
awake. Tink, who normally slept on the floor beside him and had been there when he'd gone to
sleep, wasn't there now.

"Tink?" Tim called softly. "Tink?"

An answering scratch and whimper led him to
his parents' bedroom.

The door was closed, and Tink was obviously on
the other side of it.

Tim frowned; he hadn't closed Tink in, certainly.
Why would Sarah have?

He opened the door. Tink bounded out, wagging and leaping, but then glanced nervously back
at the trapdoor.

"The bat flew up into the attic," Tim reassured
him, rubbing his ears, "and we closed the trapdoor
after him. Come on." He headed for his own room
again; Tink trotted after him and lay down in his
usual place.

Yawning, and mad at Sarah for closing Tink up,
Tim went back to bed.

chapter 9

Butterflies

He woke to a crying Jenny tugging on his bed-clothes.

"Warizzit?" he managed to say; it had taken him a while to get back to sleep after his dream, and he was, he now found, in a rotten temper.

"Sarah won't wake up!" Jenny sobbed. "I spilled some milk. I want Mommy. When's Mommy coming home?"

Tim groaned and looked at his clock; 10:25 already! It hadn't been *that* hard a night!

"Mommy's coming as soon as she can," he said, getting up and thinking glumly that even Aunt Clara might be better than this. "Where's Tink?" he asked as he pulled a sweatshirt on over his pajamas; it was a cool morning even for coastal Maine. A glance out his window showed him why: a thick fog lay over the bay.

"Eating the milk." Jenny sniffed loudly. "There isn't any more."

Tim groaned again. That would mean a trip to the store. He handed Jenny a tissue. "Well, come on," he said, trying to sound cheerful. "Let's get Sarah up and then we'll all have some toast."

"I want cereal." Jenny's eyes brimmed over once more.

Tim put his hands on her shoulders. "Jenny, you can't have cereal if there's no milk. Toast is just as good, and we can drink orange juice. We'll have cereal tomorrow, when we get more milk. Or maybe we could have cereal for lunch."

"Want peanut butter for lunch."

"Okay, you can have peanut butter then. Now come on. We need you to be a big girl while Mommy and Daddy are away. Can you be a big girl?"

Tearfully, Jenny nodded, and took Tim's hand as he led her across the hall.

There was no motion from Sarah's bed. In fact, Sarah was just a shapeless lump under the covers, which were bunched up around her neck.

"Sarah?" Tim went to her while Jenny stood in the doorway.

She didn't move.

"Sar'?" He was at her bedside now, and he looked

down uneasily at the little he could see of her. This was unlike her. It was usually Sarah who was first up, bouncy and full of plans—not to mention orders—for the new day.

Tim bent down and pulled the covers away, noticing as he did so that she seemed to have spilled brownish-red paint on her pillow. It's probably something to do with her butterfly collection, he thought. There were a couple of new specimens next to the pins and the chloroform bottle on her night table.

"Sarah," he said again, shaking her. "Wake up. It's morning—almost lunchtime. Come on, *wake up!*" He shook her harder, now seriously alarmed.

At last Sarah's eyes opened slowly, and before they seemed to focus, she reached up and grabbed at the air, saying, "Oh, what a beauty! Oh, come— come—let me see . . ." Then her eyes did seem to focus, first on the empty air and then on Tim, and she dropped her arm.

"I must have been dreaming," she said apologetically, turning toward the butterflies on her night table. "One, two . . . but there were a lot more." She frowned and looked around the room—up high, Tim noticed, not on the floor where you would normally look for something you'd lost.

"More what?" he asked.

"More butterflies," she said. "Oh, Tim," she went

on, her eyes shining now. "There were so many, so many beautiful ones, ones I'd never seen before—a bright blue one, with green spots, and one that was all yellow and red—he was huge—and then a tiny brown one—but the brown was just his veins, I think. His wings were transparent; you could see right through them . . ."

"Sarah," said Tim, "what are you talking about?"

"No butterflies," Jenny said solemnly, coming in and sitting on the foot of Sarah's bed. "There weren't any butterflies, Sarah."

"There were so. Last night, all over our room."

"No," said Jenny.

Sarah scratched her head. "Butterflies," she said softly. Then she looked at Tim as if she didn't quite believe herself. "The room was full of them. Really." She got up and ran to the window, examining the screen.

Tim and Jenny followed her, and she showed them where a corner of the screen had come out of its frame. "They must've come in here," she said. "I bet it was some kind of migration. Monarchs migrate." She went to her bookcase and pulled out a thick book with a butterfly on the cover.

Tim took the book from her gently. "After breakfast," he said. "I'm starved. So's Jenny."

"I spilled the milk," Jenny said sadly. "Tink ate it all up."

"Drank it," Sarah corrected absently, taking the book back and flipping pages. "You drink liquids, Jenny. You eat solids."

"Sarah . . ." began Tim.

"You go. I'll be there in a minute. I'm not hungry anyway."

Reluctantly—for something was clearly not right with Sarah, Tim knew—Tim took Jenny by the hand and led her downstairs. Tink had cleaned up the milk as well as any mop could, and seemed overjoyed to be let out. But he ran around the cabin, Tim noticed, nose to the ground as if tracking something, and his hackles were up.

Around lunchtime, when the fog had lifted and his late breakfast had settled in his stomach, Tim went out for a run, leaving Sarah and Jenny at home weeding the garden and looking for butterflies. He left Tink at home, too, not wanting to think about anything but the Iron Boy. Visualization, Coach had said; picturing yourself winning was an important part of mental training. Luckily, Tim did that easily—maybe too easily, he told himself, remembering his dream the night before—but it still wouldn't hurt to practice.

He jogged up the driveway just to get away, then stopped and did a few stretches. When his muscles felt long and strong, he eased out onto the main road, building speed slowly but surely, and ignoring the cars and campers that sped past. Traffic was getting heavier, but it wasn't anywhere near as bad as it would be in July and August. Even so, it was annoying and the exhaust was unpleasant, so Tim turned down a side road he hadn't yet been on this summer, then lengthened his stride and surged. Surge—easy—surge—easy—he ran that way, alternating fast and slow, till he got to the beach at the end of the road, and there he allowed himself to stop, shading his eyes from the early-afternoon sun and looking out to sea.

Spool Island was still shrouded in mist, though Hedgehog and Horseshoe were clearly visible, and Tim could see three or four sailboats near the horizon, along with a lobster boat. It would be great to be out there, he thought, glad that they'd be going the next day.

He turned and got back to work, running along the rest of the road, which looped back to the main road, and then he went on to Blue Loon Lake. By that time he was hot, so he shucked off his shirt, jogged along the shore awhile to cool down, and plunged in. He was still so hot that the chilly water felt wonderful as he swam lazily to the center, turned, and, training now, swam fast back. Wish I had my bike, he thought, wondering if it would be safe to leave it on the shore sometime—maybe on the weekend. Once a week, he wanted to put all three sports together in the order he'd have to do them in the race: first a swim, next a bike ride, and finally a run. That way he'd get used to using the different muscles as he'd have to use them then. Not every day; Coach had said that would be too much. But surely it wouldn't hurt to do it once a week . . .

Coach.

As he finished his swim and ran back out to the main road, he wondered if he'd see that guy Mr. B again. Probably not, he decided, trying to shrug off the disappointment he felt. Hey, he said to himself, who wants to train at night anyway? And that Mr. B sure is weird!

By the time Tim got home, his bad mood had turned into a good one, and it improved even more when he saw the Gibsons' car parked in the driveway.

But then his spirits plummeted again. If the adult Gibsons were visiting, they might have found out that the adult Hoskinses weren't at the cabin—and that Aunt Clara wasn't there either.

chapter 10

What's Going On?

"So," Sarah was saying primly to Mrs. Gibson, who was on the sofa with a sleepy-looking Emily beside her, "I'm not sure when they'll be back, but . . . Oh, hi, Tim!"

"Um——hi," Tim said, pulling his eyes away from Emily, who looked paler than she had before.

In order to avoid saying something about their parents that would contradict whatever Sarah had said, Tim went out into the kitchen and leaned against the counter. Milk, he thought absently; we've got to get milk.

Snatches of conversation drifted in to him, and then the porch door opened and shut. A few seconds later, Sarah joined him, rubbing her head as if she, too, was tired.

"What did you tell her?" Tim asked.

"Sort of the truth, that Mom and Dad were called away to Grandpa's suddenly. I didn't mention Aunt Clara."

Tim nodded. "She say anything?"

"Just that we should call her if we need anything. And she invited us for dinner tomorrow, after we go to the islands."

"Good," Tim said unenthusiastically. He wondered why he wasn't more excited; he'd been looking forward to going, but now he had an odd sense of dread about it.

"Emily's gotten even weirder," Sarah said after a minute. "You know, it's funny . . ."

"What's funny?"

Sarah shook her head, but then said, "She was talking about her rabbit dream again, so I told her my butterfly one. She sort of stared at me and then she said that mine sounded like her first rabbit dream—lots of rabbits, beautiful ones, all over her room. Only now it's usually just one rabbit, and I think she's scared of it."

"Scared? Of a *rabbit*? How come?"

"I don't know. But it's so weird that she said my dream's like hers."

Tim nodded.

"Tim . . ." Sarah began, then paused. "What's going on?" she whispered, even as Tim was about to ask the same question.

74

But Tim had no answer, either for himself or for her.

While Sarah took Jenny to the beach to look for interesting pebbles, Tim biked to the village for the milk. But he forgot to get anything for dinner when he was there, so they improvised with canned tuna fish, lettuce, popcorn, and ice cream. Later, in case Mr. B might be there after all, Tim biked out to the main road, without Tink this time. It was just getting dark, and fog was snaking in from the bay. Tim hoped they weren't about to be socked in with it again, for if they were, Mr. Gibson would probably veto the next day's trip to the islands.

"Good evening!"

Tim lurched, startled; even though he'd been thinking about Mr. B, the man and his bike appeared so silently that Tim had no warning—no whirr of wheels, no crunch of gravel.

"I am sorry," Mr. B said gravely, "that I was unable to be seeing you last evening. I had, I am afraid, business I could not avoid."

"That's okay," Tim said, more pleased than he'd expected to be that Mr. B hadn't stood him up intentionally. "Only is there a phone number or something where I could reach you? I was almost late myself. You could call me if you can't come—555-9435. And I could call you if I can't come. What's your number?"

"It's 555-987—but no," Mr. B said. "That—er—that will not—how do you say?—do it. I am not having any telephone where I am living."

That seemed odd; why had he started to give a number then? And why did the number seem familiar?

But then all the numbers in Starfish Harbor began with 555. And maybe what he'd started to give was his work number.

"I could try to call during business hours," Tim suggested. "Was that your work number?"

Mr. B shook his head. "It is not a good idea. They will not wish me to be telephoning."

"Well, okay," Tim said. "I'll just try to be here every night on time. Or—look, if I can't come, I'll tie a piece of string on the tree here." He gestured to a small fir by the side of the road. "If you see a string here, that means I can't come."

Mr. B nodded, and for the next hour or so, they rode side by side, bike lights illuminating the road ahead. Mr. B held Tim's flashlight on him, watching his form. "You do not bend low enough," he announced at the very beginning of their session, and Tim figured that was true; at least Coach had mentioned it often enough. He thought he'd improved, though, and maybe he had, but it was good to have a check on it. Mr. B seemed to know a lot about wind resistance and drafting and aerodynamics. Tim was impressed, and impressed with his speed, too, for Mr. B easily outstripped him in a couple of short races along the road. "You can be building endurance in the daytime," Mr. B told him. "But at night, we will be doing speed work, I think, and gradually you will be going faster as well as farther, eh?"

"Sure," Tim said breathlessly; Mr. B had just beaten him in an especially rapid sprint. He held out his hand to shake Mr. B's. Who cares about weird, he thought. This is one good coach!

Mr. B's grip was strong, but his hand was surprisingly cold against Tim's hot, sweaty one. In fact, Tim was so startled by it that he drew back his own hand involuntarily.

Mr. B's eyes narrowed. "I am having a—er—a disorder of the blood circulation," he explained. "I am often forgetting that my hands, to most people, feel so cold. I am sorry I was—er—surprising you."

"Oh, that's okay," Tim said, embarrassed.

"Until tomorrow then? Tomorrow we will work on the running, yes? And then soon, when the moon is full, we will be swimming. You must tell me where we can swim."

"Blue Loon Lake. We can bike there from here easily."

"Very good," said Mr. B with a little dip of his head. "Until tomorrow then."

He sprang onto his bike and rode off.

The fog, Tim realized happily as he biked home, seemed to be going rapidly back out to sea.

Sarah looked up languidly from her butterfly book when Tim came in; she yawned. "Mom called again."

"Oh? How's Grandpa?"

"Better. Mom said he recognized them—Granny and Mom and Dad. And he smiled and squeezed their hands. It must be awful not to be able to talk, though." Sarah yawned again.

"Yeah." Tim sat down opposite her, patting Tink absently. "It must be. Maybe by the time we're that old, they'll have figured out how to make people live forever."

Sarah seemed to cringe. "I'm not sure I'd like that."

"Oh, I don't know," said Tim. Then he grinned. "I'm surprised you're so negative about it. Vampires"—he bent closer to Sarah and bared his teeth—"live forever."

"Don't!" she said sharply, recoiling. "Don't kid about it. Besides, they don't really live forever. They're undead, not alive. It's not funny, Tim."

He stared at her. "Sheesh," he said. "I didn't mean anything. Lighten up, can't you? What'd you say about Aunt Clara?"

"That she was out visiting a neighbor."

"Not good. She'd never leave us alone at night."

"I know. I said the neighbor was sick."

"Better, but feeble."

"Why don't you make a list of good excuses, Mr. Know-Everything?" Sarah said angrily around another yawn. "The next time she calls I'll just read one of them off."

"Sorry. Is there any more ice cream?"

"A little. I thought you were in training."

Tim went into the kitchen. "Yeah," he called, "but I'm also hungry. That Mr. B guy's pretty fast." He peered around the corner at her. "Want some?"

Sarah made a face. "No." She slammed her book shut. "I'm going to bed. Good night." And she yawned once more, hugely.

That's odd, thought Tim, taking his bowl out to the porch and eating the ice cream slowly with Tink beside him, obviously waiting for the last lick. Sarah's always hungry.

His feet ached and his chest felt as if it would split open, but he was hardly aware of either as he pounded along the road, oblivious to the other runners, to the sounds of his feet and his own breathing, to the sweat cooling and drying on his saturated clothes. In his mind he saw only the road ahead and the tape—the tape that he would soon break with his chest if he could just keep up this punishing, inhuman pace . . .

79

"Mommy! Mommy!"

That was Jenny. Tim's eyes flew open, and he was out of bed and running for the girls' room before he was fully awake.

Jenny met him at the door, crying hysterically. "Mommy, Mommy, Mommy!"

"Shh, Jen, she's not here," Tim said, picking her up awkwardly. "Tim's here. It's okay, Jenny, it'll be okay. What's the matter?"

"S-S-Sarah. It's Sarah. She's—she's walking around, but she won't talk to me. She—she looks funny. I'm scared. I want MOMMY!"

"Okay, Jenny." Tim put her down next to Tink, who had padded along after him and was standing there watching anxiously. "You hold on to Tink's collar and stay right here. Tink, sit. Stay," he commanded firmly, and went into his sisters' room.

Sarah was at the window, methodically trying to rip the screen the rest of the way off its frame.

"Sarah?" he asked cautiously, going to her. "Sarah, for Pete's sake, what're you doing?"

She ignored him. Her eyes were fully open and she looked right at him, but if she saw him, she made no sign of recognition. There was an odd smile on her face, and he could now see that she held her butterfly net in one hand—which must be why, he thought, she's having such a time with the screen. But why not just open it, and why would she want it open in the first place?

"Sarah," he said again, softly this time, taking her hand gently, moving it away from the screen—

And then, outside, he saw it: a giant butterfly, pale green and translucent, hovering in front of the window, looking in at Sarah with small golden eyes—glittering eyes, cold as ice . . .

chapter 11

Spool Island

"It was a luna moth, not a butterfly," Sarah said, sitting up in bed and hugging her knees as she sipped the hot chocolate Tim had made for her. Jenny had finished hers and was asleep again, curled up next to Tink on her own bed. "A big, beautiful luna moth."

"Too big for your collection, Sarah," Tim pointed out, still shaken by the experience. No moth could be that big, he knew; the size of an eagle, almost!

"Was it?" Sarah said vaguely. "This cocoa hurts my throat." She put the mug down and rubbed her neck. "Maybe I'm getting a cold. I'm so tired!"

"Sarah," said Tim, "come on now, tell me about it before you fall asleep again."

She frowned. "It's a little mixed up. I—I had

that dream again, I think. You know, with all the
butterflies. Then they all went away, but I knew—
you know how you know things in dreams—I knew
there was one outside the window, the best one of
all, and so I went to let it in."

"How come you were trying to take the screen
off its frame instead of just opening it?"

"It was stuck. I couldn't get it open."

"Is that it? The whole story?"

"That's it." She smiled ruefully. "I'm almost sorry
you found me."

"And have that huge insect in the house? You
were upset about a few bats, for Pete's sake!"

"I know. But bats aren't beautiful."

"I bet they are to other bats." Tim paused for a
moment, waiting for Sarah to laugh. When she
didn't, he said, "Sarah, *think*. A moth that big just
isn't possible."

"No," she said softly. "No, I guess not. But we
both saw it. And—oh, no!"

"What?"

Sarah now looked frightened for the first time.
"Emily," she whispered. "Emily said the rabbit that
comes to her is big—as big as a dog."

"But Emily's dreaming the rabbits, right? And
we both saw the moth. I can't have been dreaming, too."

"I— Yeah, you're right. But maybe we'd better
talk to Emily anyway. Tim?"

"What?"

"Maybe it's all part of—you know."

"Of what?"

"Of whatever's going on."

Except for Emily, everything seemed pretty normal the next morning when Tim and Sarah and Jenny met John by the town dock. "Emily's feeling rotten," John told them, "and she won't get out of bed. She looks so awful I bet Mom wouldn't let her get up anyway, even if she wanted to." He heaved a huge picnic basket into the dinghy.

"How are her dreams?" Sarah asked with a significant glance at Tim, who'd already gotten aboard. She handed Jenny down to him and then got in herself.

"About the same, I guess. She doesn't talk about them anymore. But"—John cast off and jumped aboard—"I guess she still has them. I hear her talking in her sleep sometimes, like she's scared."

Sarah glanced at Tim again, and then looked back at John. "What do you mean?" she asked.

John hoisted the dinghy's mainsail after gesturing to Tim to take the tiller. "I don't know. She just sounds scared, that's all. A couple of times I've heard her say 'Oh, no!' and 'Don't!' Things like that. Hey, it's too nice a day to talk about Emily's problems."

"You're right," Tim said, and they set about the

business of guiding the dinghy out of the crowded harbor—Tim and John did anyway; no one expected Jenny to help, and Sarah looked too preoccupied to pay much attention to sailing.

They sailed past lobster boats and charter fishing boats, huge fancy yachts and battered, hardworking dories. Then they glided smoothly between the buoys and out into the bay, making for Horseshoe Island, closest in and their first stop. The sun was warm, the water calm, the wind just right, and there was no sign of fog.

"I've got another gig coming up tomorrow," John said casually. "Another kids' party. Want to come?"

"Sure," Tim agreed eagerly. "Sarah?"

"Okay," she answered listlessly. She'd been trailing her hand in the water—unlike her, Tim realized. Normally, old Take-Charge Sarah would be impatient for her turn at the tiller, and critical of whoever was handling it.

"Me too!" said Jenny. "I want to see more magic!"

John laughed and tousled Jenny's hair. "My biggest fan, huh? Okay. I'm sure I can get the hostess to accept her as one of the guests," he added to Tim and Sarah. "Whoops! Ready about!"

Tim waited, alert. He hadn't sailed since last summer, and he always felt a little rusty the first time. But he was ready when John said, "Hard alee!" He pushed the tiller over right on time and ducked under the boom as it swung across. The sail filled again, on the other side, and the dinghy sped off on a port tack.

"Nice breeze," John observed. "We can make for land on the next tack, I bet."

They did, reaching the island and beaching the dinghy in record time.

Horseshoe was so named because it was long and narrow, and curved around a small bay which was nestled between the two prongs of the "shoe." No one lived there, and there were only a few trees, on the highest part, right in the middle. Mostly, Horseshoe was a sand bar, but there were often good shells on its beach, and interesting bones and bits of flotsam. Once, they'd come upon most of a dory, battered by a storm. There were few rocks— unusual for Maine—and a huge colony of terns. Because of them, John had asked that they leave Tink at home, explaining that terns nest on the ground and are easily disturbed by exuberant dogs.

They waded off Horseshoe's sandy beach, for the tide had just come in and the water in the island's shallow little bay was warm enough for that, though not for swimming. Then they dried off in the sun, and at last climbed back into the dinghy to head for Hedgehog, a small, round island, prickly with spruce trees. "Lunch on Hedgehog?" John asked. "I guess we shouldn't land on Spool, with those city people there."

The Hoskinses agreed, and they had a large and

lazy lunch on the rocky beach before they explored the spruce woods as they did every year. Nothing had changed, except for a few new blowdowns—trees uprooted and blown over by the storm winds that pounded the islands in the winter. "Had some bad weather," John said, and Tim laughed.

"You say that every year," he reminded John. "Every winter's worse than the last one, to hear you tell it. By the time we're grown up, there'll have been so many blowdowns that Hedgehog'll be a desert."

John laughed, too, then poked Tim and said, "Look at Sarah."

Tim looked, and stopped laughing, for Sarah, who had been gathering spruce cones with Jenny, had fallen asleep under a tree.

She woke quickly, though, when Tim shook her, and he soon forgot all about it as they sailed around Spool.

The island was called Spool because it had once boasted a sawmill and a small factory that made the giant wooden spools heavy electrical cable is wound on. The wood for the spools came from the island's trees, but eventually, when they'd all been cut down, the mill and the factory had gone out of business. For a few years, they'd opened each summer so tourists could see how the spools had been made, but that hadn't brought in enough money to support the island's handful of residents.

It wasn't long before they all died or moved away, and now the few houses, small church, factory, and sawmill looked like buildings in a ghost town.

"I can't imagine why anyone would have wanted to buy this place," John said as he headed the dinghy for the beach. "But I guess there's no figuring city people. Let's get the mainsail down, crew."

They lowered it, pulled up the centerboard, and got out the oars so they could get as close as possible to the shore.

"No boat," Tim observed as John rowed them past the rotting dock on the lee side of the island.

"Nope," said John. "Weird, isn't it? And no one's ever seen the new owner in the village buying supplies."

"Maybe he's got a private supply boat," Sarah suggested sleepily.

"If he does," John said, "no one's ever seen it."

"Maybe he doesn't live there," said Tim, thinking the island looked just as deserted as he remembered it. He tried to see beyond the dock to the tumbledown houses that they'd explored many times, but he couldn't tell if anyone was in them or in the old sawmill and factory up on the hill in the center of the island. "Who'd want to live in a ruined house?"

"I don't know." John shipped his oars and looked toward shore with them. "But Dad says that lobstermen going by have heard voices, and soon after the place was sold, a big boat anchored off the island for a few days. The weather was so stormy, though, that only one lobsterman got close enough to see anything. He told Dad it looked like some big boxes were rowed ashore."

"That was the supplies, I bet," said Tim.

"But no people," said John. "Not that anyone saw anyway."

"Look!" squealed Jenny suddenly. "Look!"

Tim followed her pointing finger to the dock and beyond. Near it, and next to a prominent No Trespassing sign, was a small wooden crate. "See?" he said. "More supplies. I bet that guy's living here after all!"

"Let's go ashore," John said decisively.

"What about the No Trespassing sign?" Tim asked.

"There doesn't seem to be anyone around," John said. "And we'll think of some excuse if there is. How about it? I could use some excitement. It's been kind of a boring spring, with Emily sick and all."

"Okay," said Tim. "Sarah?"

Sarah looked doubtful, but she didn't seem to object, and no one thought to consult Jenny.

John rowed quietly to the dock and was about to tie up, when the piling he'd thrown his line around split and tumbled into the water.

"Rotten," he said. "Like everything else here. I

89

remember thinking last year that it might go soon. Guess we'd better not try to tie up." He rowed around the dock and pulled the dinghy way up on the pebble beach.

Tim felt oddly tense as they got out of the dinghy and climbed up the bank to where the beach ended and the proper land began. When he glanced at Sarah, he was sure she was feeling the same way. Even John seemed subdued; only Jenny was bubbly, normal. She ran to the box, which Tim could see was larger than it had looked from the water.

"It's open," Jenny shouted gleefully, lifting the lid. Then she stared down into it, disappointment all over her face.

"What's in it, kittycat?" Sarah asked as she went up to Jenny.

"Good grief!" said John, getting there before Tim and looking inside.

Tim peered over his shoulder. The box, it appeared, was full of dirt.

"Well," said Sarah, "maybe they're gardeners and it's some special kind of dirt. Or—or maybe it's bulbs or plants packed in dirt." She reached out as if to dig in the box, but Tim pulled her hand away. She looked at him. "You're right," she said. "If it's rare plants, they'd be mad if we messed them up."

"Or maybe," said John in what Tim recognized as a mock serious tone, "it's some rare kind of worms."

"I'm not into that anymore," Sarah retorted crossly. She turned away. "Are we going to look around, or what?"

The three of them hesitated near the foot of the dock, where the ghost village's main street began.

"It's not as if we haven't seen it before," said Tim uneasily.

"But we haven't seen it since it's been bought," said John.

"And since all those No Trespassing signs went up," Sarah added.

"What's no tre-passing?" asked Jenny.

"It means don't go there," Tim explained.

"Where?"

"Where it says not to trespass."

"Then we shouldn't go!"

"I guess not," Tim said. "No, we probably shouldn't. But there doesn't seem to be anyone around to get mad if we do."

"Mommy wouldn't like it," Jenny said primly.

"Well, I'm going as far as the factory," John told them. "I'm just going to see if anyone's doing anything to it—you know, like making it into condos or something. City people are always doing that. You guys can stay here if you want."

"It's not that I don't want to go," said Sarah, sitting on the box, whose lid was now closed again. "It's just that I keep getting so tired." She stifled a yawn.

"Me too." Jenny sat beside her.

Tim shrugged. "What the heck?" he said, and followed John.

"I didn't want to say anything before," John told him as they trudged up the broken pavement of the road that led from the beach to the houses and the church, and then up the hill to the sawmill and factory. "But I think something fishy's going on here. I think we ought to take a look around."

"What kind of fishy?"

"You figure it out." John turned to face him. "Someone buys the place but never shows up in town; he puts No Trespassing signs up. No one sees any boats, except the one that delivered the boxes. You don't deliver boxes if nothing's going on! And if no one's around, how come people have heard voices? Now there's the box we just found, with dirt in it. Or what looks like dirt," he added darkly.

"Drugs?" asked Tim, his heart starting to pound uncomfortably.

John nodded. "There's cocaine smuggled in lots of places on the Maine coast, Dad says. Why not here?"

"You mean there might be cocaine in that box? Buried in the dirt?"

"Or might have been," said John. "I don't think they'd leave it around like that if it was still there. They've probably taken it out to sell it. Maybe"— he glanced around—"they've got a plane. Helicopter, maybe."

"Maybe," said Tim softly, "they're up at the factory, doing whatever it is people do with cocaine to get it ready to sell."

John nodded.

"But no one's seen any lights?" Tim asked as they approached the old church and its overgrown graveyard.

"Would you show a light if you were running drugs?"

"No, I guess not. Hey, look!"

There was fresh scuffed-up dirt near three of the graves, and the headstones near them were leaning, as if someone had been digging around them and had loosened them.

"Winter storms and spring rains and snow runoff," John suggested, but his voice lacked conviction. "Maybe frost heaves. They do funny things to the land."

"You don't sound like you believe that," Tim said nervously.

"I don't. Want to look?"

Tim licked his lips. "Sure," he said.

John turned toward the graveyard gate but then turned back, saying, "Maybe we should see if anyone's here first."

"Good idea," Tim agreed. They went on to the factory, walking more softly now, and not speaking at all.

The lilac and yew bushes around the factory's foundation had grown shaggier, and the roof had a few more loose and curling shingles, but everything else looked just as Tim remembered it. Even their improvised picnic table, a relic from the past, was still near the path: a single old spool with weather-beaten insulated cable wound around it. It was left over from when the sawmill and factory were open for visitors; it had been displayed so the tourists could see what the spools were actually used for.

"We'd better be quiet," John whispered to Tim, "in case the drug people are here."

Silently, the two boys tiptoed around the old building, peering into windows dark with dust and cobwebs. It was impossible to see much of anything inside, but Tim was just able to make out what seemed to be several more boxes like the one near the dock—larger, though, and longer.

"Doesn't look as if anyone's here," John whispered when they got around to the front again. "How about we go in?"

Tim felt a fluttering in his stomach, but he didn't want to seem chicken, so he nodded. With his heart pounding even harder and his mouth dry, he followed close after John as John pushed open the unlocked door—

And ran out again, fast, hands shielding his face and head, yelling something that sounded very like "ARGH!"

Tim glanced quickly behind John and then took off, too, running just as fast.

chapter 12

Flu?

"Bats!" they both shouted to Sarah and Jenny as they ran up to the dinghy and gestured to the girls to get in.

"Hundreds of bats," Tim said, pushing off. "If you thought we had a lot at our house, you should see this bunch!"

"Maybe this is where they went." John handed the oars to Tim. "Here, you row a bit—then we'll sail. Your bats had to go somewhere."

"Mices," said Jenny happily. "*Our* bat mices!"

"Yuck." Sarah looked anxiously over her shoulder. "No thanks!"

Tim put the oars in the oarlocks as fast as he could, and now the sky along the shore turned black with bats. The sound of their agitated, high-pitched squeaking followed the dinghy as he rowed steadily away. "There's your voices, maybe," he said to John when at last it looked as if the bats weren't going to chase them all the way home. "The bats' squeaking."

John nodded.

Dinner with the Gibsons was quiet, mostly because of Emily, who didn't seem interested in hearing about their island trip, and was so listless she seemed to be making everyone else feel listless, too. At least Tim felt that way, and he noticed that Sarah, especially, talked very little and just picked at her food. Finally, when dessert was served—a huge chocolate cake with goopy frosting—Emily pushed her chair back, looking a little green, and said, "May I be excused?"

"You've hardly eaten . . ." began Mrs. Gibson, but Mr. Gibson put his hand over hers and said, "Okay, Emily, honey. But remember your new pills."

"We took her to the doctor again yesterday," Mrs. Gibson explained. "He says she's still anemic—if anything, a little more so. He's given her stronger iron pills plus some antibiotics." She looked after her daughter anxiously. "I sure hope they work!"

"Me too, Mrs. Gibson," Tim said, eyeing the cake. Exerting all the willpower he could muster, he said, "May I be excused, too? I've got to meet my coach, and I'd better not fill up on cake if I'm going to be any good for him at all."

"Coach?" asked Mr. Gibson.

Tim explained briefly about Mr. B, and then, while the others—except for Sarah—tucked into the cake with a vengeance, he said goodbye and left.

He'd brought his bike and his running clothes to the Gibsons', so all he had to do now was change, hop on, and ride to the meeting place. It was a warm night—almost too warm for running, Tim thought, pedaling rapidly along the road. The fog was coming in, too; funny the way it seemed to arrive every night at around this time . . .

Again Mr. B appeared without warning, clad in his black running shorts and the black T-shirt with its red stripe. Suddenly Tim remembered his dream—and the guy in it; hadn't he been dressed sort of the same way? He stared nervously.

"Good evening," said Mr. B with his usual formal nod. "You are being a little later than last time, no?"

"No. I—I mean yes. Sorry. I had to go to dinner at a friend's house. The Gibsons." Then he realized Mr. B probably wouldn't know them.

"The Gibsons," said Mr. B, his eyes narrowing. "Yes. John and the young Emily, I believe?"

"Yes, that's right," said Tim, surprised. He added awkwardly, "So I guess you *are* from around here. I wasn't sure."

Mr. B smiled vaguely, with his lips closed, and Tim realized how rarely—if ever—he'd seen him smile. "I have been here for a while," Mr. B said. "With my—er—business."

"What is your business?" Tim asked curiously.

"It is varied. Many small . . . services. Now, shall we be starting the run? Let me see your form first. Run past me, please, up and down the road. I will use your so excellent flashlight again if I may, although"—he glanced up at the sky—"the moon is nearly full. Tomorrow, I think, we swim."

Tim set off down the road, and this time it was unnecessary motion Mr. B told him he should work on—too much thrust with his right leg, a little fluttering of his left hand. Again, his school coach had said the same things.

"Sheesh," Tim said at the end of the session, rubbing his sweaty face with a black towel Mr. B produced from a small bag he had with him. "It's like I still have all the same problems I had at school."

"But perhaps," said Mr. B, "you have them less than before, eh? It is easy to be falling into bad habits, is it not so, when there is no one watching you." He gave a little bow. "This is why I can be being of use to you. But now it is late, and we must part." He smiled again, and this time Tim got a brief glimpse of large yellow teeth in the moonlight and caught a whiff of stale breath; he moved

98

away a little. "Remember," said Mr. B as he turned away toward the shore road—on foot tonight, Tim realized, not seeing his bike—"tomorrow you will show me the swimming place, and we will swim."

"You'll need to bring your bike," Tim called after him.

Mr. B turned and waved, then turned away again. I hope he heard me, Tim thought, getting on his own bike and riding off in the opposite direction.

Again, the fog now seemed to be heading out to sea.

Tim woke just before dawn, hearing a strange scrabbling sound and a low growl from Tink. He sat up and rubbed his eyes, then realized the sound seemed to be coming from the girls' room. "Come on, Tink," he said sleepily, climbing out of bed and heading into the hall—but Tink stopped outside the girls' door. The hair on his neck stood straight up and his growl became a snarl.

"What is it?" Tim asked softly. "Tink?" A small knot of fear formed itself inside Tim's stomach as he slowly opened the door and went in. Tink, his legs planted firmly on the floor, refused to join him.

Everything seemed peaceful; both girls were sound asleep, their covers pulled up around their shoulders. Sarah's were bunched tightly around her throat, in fact. Jenny moaned a little in her sleep and tossed, and Tim, fearing he'd wake her, stopped

99

near the door. He could still hear the sound, faintly, by the window, so he looked toward it—and saw the screen, ripped all the way out of its frame and lying on the floor.

Quickly, he went to the window and looked out. He thought for a moment he saw a flash of green wings—the luna moth again?—but it was gone as soon as he saw it, and then the sun broke through the morning mist over the bay.

Jenny moaned again and muttered something in her sleep that sounded like "Pretty flutterby." Tink, tail wagging now, came into the room and sniffed her. When he got to Sarah's bed, though, he whimpered and gave it a wide berth.

"Go back to sleep, Jenny," Tim whispered as Jenny sat up, her curls cascading in tangles over her shoulders.

"Where's my flutterby?" she asked sleepily.

"What butterfly?" Tim whispered. "Shh—don't wake Sarah."

"I had a flutterby," Jenny said. "Just for me, not Sarah's."

"When?"

"Last night." Jenny smiled. "It was sooo pretty! It was littler than Sarah's, and it said that's coz I'm littler. But it was my very own one. Oh, I wish it would come back!" She fell back against the pillow and closed her eyes.

"Did you understand that?" Tim said to Tink as they left the room. "Is everyone crazy except us? Come on, boy, we might as well go for a run or something before breakfast."

Early that afternoon, when Sarah was reading a story to Jenny on the porch, John came over and said that his party had been canceled because the child it was for was sick. "Sounds like what Emily's got," he told Tim, looking puzzled. "No energy, funny dreams. Like the little kid who couldn't go to the party you went to, remember? He had pretty much the same symptoms. I wonder if it's some kind of flu."

"If it is, I think Sarah's got it. And maybe Jenny. At least she's having dreams now. Maybe we're next," Tim said, only half joking. "How do you feel?"

John shrugged and reached down to Tink, who was pawing him, asking to be patted. "Fine, I guess. I'm sorry about the party, though. I was going to do a new trick. It's a knot that can't be untied except, of course, by Gibson the Great." He made a sweeping bow, then said, "Oh, I almost forgot. Emily wants to see Sarah."

"How come?" Tim asked, surprised. "She didn't seem to want to talk to anyone last night."

"I don't know. She said it was very important, though. Whew!" John wiped his forehead. "It's hot today. Maybe it's just as well the party's been canceled. This might be the one day of the year when I swim in the bay. Water temp's up, I heard."

"Yeah?" Tim said, glad to think about something else. "Hey, maybe I'll join you—do my cold-water training. The Iron Boy's in the ocean, so I ought to get used to it."

"You sure should," John told him, "if the water where you'll be is anything like as cold as the water usually is here."

"It's not. It's off Cape Cod, a lot warmer than here, at least on the side of the Cape the race is on. Coach says I should do most of my training in the lake but go into the bay once in a while when it's human. You know, warm."

"Well," said John, "it's human today, I think. Want to go now?"

"Sure," Tim answered, figuring he could use a little extra practice before swimming with Mr. B. He didn't want to make a fool of himself in front of his new coach. "Let me just tell Sarah about Emily. Then you're on!"

chapter 13

Disaster—Almost!

Despite what John had said, the water in the bay was still cold enough to take a little getting used to. Even so, it was fine when they'd been in it for a while, and Tim decided he'd suggest to Mr. B that he train in the bay that night, too. Why not seize the opportunity while he had it? Besides, maybe Mr. B could give him some extra tips on saltwater swimming. He found he was really looking forward to his session with him. After all, Mr. B had already given him some pretty good pointers.

When Tim got back to the cabin after his swim with John, he found Sarah sitting on the sofa in the Big Room, with books spread out all over the cushions, as if she were doing one of those research projects she was so good at in school. Jenny was playing roll-the-ball with Tink on the porch.

"Hi," Tim called, turning into the kitchen.

There was no answer from Sarah, so he went into the Big Room. "Hi," he said again.

Sarah silently turned a page and then scribbled something on a pad of paper.

Tim cupped his hands around his mouth, went up to Sarah, and shouted in her ear. "HI!"

"You don't have to yell," Sarah said irritably, scratching at what looked like a couple of big mosquito bites on her neck. "I heard you."

"Then how come you didn't answer?"

"Because I'm reading."

"Some excuse." Tim picked up one of the books and looked at the title. "*Folklore and Myth*, huh? Since when are you interested in that?"

"Since I talked to Emily." Sarah made another note.

He looked at the book she was reading. "Oh, good grief. Are you back to that stuff again?" The book was called *The Vampire in Fact and Fiction*. Tim clapped his hand to his forehead in mock long-suffering anguish. "Next thing you know, you'll be putting on those long teeth again and going around in a cape. What's wrong with butterflies?"

"Tim, do you mind?" Sarah said crossly. "I'm trying to figure something out. There's some cans of clam chowder for dinner," she added. "It's your turn to cook."

Mr. B agreed to swim in the bay that night. The weather was still and humid, though a wind was coming up, and the full moon shone weakly through the mist. Here and there, bits of quartz on the rocks along the cabin's little beach sparkled in its light.

Tim shivered as he walked into the water; it was colder than it had been that afternoon. Mr. B, though, didn't seem to mind—and he's so thin, Tim thought, that he doesn't have any insulation at all. Not just thin; athlete or no athlete, he looked positively unhealthy in his black bathing suit. His skin was as white as the underbelly of a dead frog Tim had once seen.

"So," said Mr. B, "we are swimming out to where we are opposite that little point with the tall tree, yes? And then we are swimming back. Then we will be talking about your form, and then we will be working."

"Okay," Tim said, measuring the distance: perhaps an eighth of a mile each way. Child's play.

But the cold water sapped his energy and tightened his muscles, and he found himself gasping a little at first and wondering why Mr. B hadn't let him warm up—why he hadn't insisted on it himself, in fact. And now the wind was getting stronger.

It would feel cold on his wet body when he stopped swimming—but no, it was a warm wind. By the time Tim made the turn opposite the point, though, the wind was kicking up waves. Maybe this isn't such a great idea after all, he thought.

"Good," Mr. B said when they returned to their starting place. "Your form is excellent. But you should be cutting the water a little more—how do you say? sharp? clean? like a knife?—with your hand, and bending your knees perhaps a little bit more when you are kicking. But it is good, very good." He smiled and Tim tried not to be obvious about moving away from his bad breath. "Now," said Mr. B, "we will be doing some speed work. Once again to opposite the point and back. Do not be thinking about the waves; they are good practice for you, yes? Suppose there are waves on the race day, eh? Just go as fast as you can; I am keeping up, I think."

It was hard to ignore the waves, though; they were getting steadily bigger. They were whitecaps now, in fact, and their foam glowed eerily in the misty moonlight.

But what the heck, Tim thought grimly. He's right; what if there are waves on race day? I'll just pretend they aren't there and go as fast as I can— he plunged in—but I'm not sure I'll be able to go at anywhere near my usual speed . . .

He pulled ahead of Mr. B, who was swimming beside him.

Of course, he thought, I won't use all my strength in the Iron Boy swim the way I'm using it now. I'll have to save some for the bike ride and the run—

Suddenly a huge wave washed over him, filling his mouth, his eyes, his nose with stinging, salty water. He struggled against it, but he was quickly disoriented. Which way is up? he wondered in silent panic, thrashing wildly, losing time.

At last his head broke the surface and he opened his mouth to spit out the water, only to be caught by another, bigger wave.

This time when he came up, he looked frantically around for Mr. B, but couldn't see him anywhere. Now his left calf muscle was tightening, cramping—and another wave was coming. Tim felt himself being swept forward by it and tried to relax, ride it in, but by then his lungs were bursting and his eyes were smarting and he wanted desperately to cough. But he was underwater again and couldn't, and he felt as if his chest were going to explode . . .

The next thing Tim knew, he was lying on the shore in the moonlight. There was a terrible smell. He opened his eyes to see Mr. B bending over him, looking not worried, as one might expect, Tim

107

thought dimly, but—joyful, almost. Yes, joyful, for he was smiling, his yellowish teeth gleaming, tinged, Tim now saw, with red, and distorted in the moonlight, for they seemed larger, longer, than they could possibly be.

Tim coughed and gagged, bringing up sea water.

"Good." Mr. B rolled him onto his side and thumped him on the back. "Good. You are being all right now."

Tim sat up. The sea was calm again, as if there had never been any wind.

"How do you feel?" asked Mr. B.

"Dizzy. My throat hurts. My leg hurts."

"Which leg? A cramp?"

"Left," Tim told him. "Yes, it cramped when I was swimming. When those waves came."

"Lie back," Mr. B ordered. "Relax. I will be rubbing it."

Tim did as he was told; he felt too weak to do anything else. It was all very weird, but he didn't seem to be able to think about it clearly, to remember it, even. Mr. B must have pulled him out, given him CPR or something, and he must have gotten bashed against the rocks while he was still in the water. At least there seemed to be scrapes on his arms, his chest, his neck.

"Did you pull me out?" he asked weakly.

"Yes."

"Thank you."

"You are welcome." Mr. B gave his leg a little pat. "How is the cramp feeling now?"

"Much better," Tim answered.

"If you can be walking on it, you should go home now. You need to rest. Here." Mr. B held out his hand and helped Tim to his feet. "I will be walking with you to the cabin—there, steady."

Tim had swayed as soon as he'd stood; he felt dizzy and, oh, so sleepy, sleepier than he'd ever been, surely. It was pleasant, sort of, or would have been if he'd only been home in bed . . .

They weren't far from the cabin, just a little way down the beach. It's a good thing, too, Tim thought as Mr. B helped him up the beach path and then up the cabin steps; I couldn't make it very far.

"Thanks," he managed to say at the door. "You probably saved my life. Thanks." He knew he should say more—saving someone's life was a pretty big deal, and Mr. B sure had been nice afterwards, rubbing his leg and all—but he was too tired, too groggy, to think of the words. Clumsily, he held out his hand, and Mr. B grasped it, then opened the door for him and gave him a little shove inside.

The momentum carried him into the Big Room, where Sarah was sitting on the couch again, poring over the same books she'd been taking notes from when Tim had left.

But when he came in, she looked up at him and screamed.

Sarah's Warning

Tim didn't have the strength to do more than stagger to a chair and collapse in it. He had enough strength, though, to wish Sarah could be a little more sympathetic. Her reaction made him wish again that their parents were home.

Sarah stopped screaming quickly, but she went on staring at him, her face white. Finally she pointed a shaking finger at his neck and gasped, "What—where—not you, too!"

Wearily, Tim struggled to his feet. "I got caught in some big waves. I almost drowned. Mr. B saved my life. Don't tell Mom if she calls. I'm going to bed."

Sarah leaped off the sofa and seized his arm. "Wait," she said. "It—it's your neck."

"My *neck!*" he exclaimed angrily. "My neck's fine. A little sore, maybe, but no more than the rest of me. It's my *life* we're talking about."

"I know," Sarah said soberly. "Mine too. Look." She pulled down the collar of her shirt and pointed to the mosquito bites he'd noticed earlier—two reddish-pink bumps.

Tim was unmoved. "Mosquitoes. Maine's known for them. Don't be a hypochondriac, Sarah."

"Oh, Tim, you don't understand. These aren't mosquito bites. They're VAMPIRE bites. Jenny has them, too; I checked. And so does Emily. Jenny's are pretty faint, but Emily's are huge and ugly; she said the doctor thinks they're infected spider bites. That's why he's giving her those antibiotics, but they aren't getting any better. And now you've got them." She touched his neck gently. "Yours are small like Jenny's, but fresher. The blood's still drying on them; that's why I could see them so easily."

Tim sat down again, his head reeling. He didn't want to believe Sarah, but he couldn't help remembering how Mr. B had bent over him, his teeth gleaming—his teeth? Oh, no, his *teeth!* Large . . . long . . . stained . . .

Why had the sea gotten calm so quickly after he'd almost drowned? And why had it also been calm before he'd started swimming?

And why did Mr. B insist on coaching him at

night, after dark? Could his job really be so demanding that he couldn't at least work in the early evening, before sunset? After all, it stayed light pretty late now!

"Maybe," Tim said unsteadily to Sarah, "you'd better begin at the beginning."

Sarah sat down again, too. "When I went to see Emily today, she was in terrible shape. She was crying, but she said she had to tell me something I wasn't going to believe. She said the rabbit in her dream doesn't seem to be in her dream anymore, but seems real. And it's been like that, she said, for a long time. She said it sort of pretends to cuddle, but it bites her on the neck, every night, and she can't seem to move when it's there, like it's hypnotized her or something. That's why she's so weak, she thinks. She . . ." Sarah paused, then went on modestly. "She said she wanted to tell me because since I used to like vampires and am good at research and stuff, maybe I wouldn't laugh at her like the grownups would, and maybe I could look up things about vampires for her. And she said she was scared for me, too, because of my butterfly dream."

Part of Tim felt an absurd desire to laugh; it all sounded like something out of a book or a movie. But the other part of him felt chilled and—yes— scared. "And?" was all he managed to say.

"Well, of course, vampires can only come out at night. And I remembered that they—like Dracula—can turn into other things. You know, become wolves or bats or mist. Or anything else they want to become."

Tim heard himself make a choking sound. He thought of the fog that came each night at the same time as Mr. B, and left when he left.

"And of course vampires suck people's blood at night and make them feel sick and weak, and eventually the people die and become vampires themselves. I didn't have to look that up to remember it."

"Bats," whispered Tim, thinking about Dracula and about what Sarah had just said about vampires turning into other things. "All those bats upstairs."

Sarah nodded. "I don't think all of them were vampires, exactly. But—but I think maybe those exterminator guys were. We only saw one of them leave, Tim. One thing I just found out from these books"—she waved her hand at the pile beside her—"is that a vampire has to be invited into a person's house, at least the first time. After that, it sort of puts a spell on its victim. Like—like the moth did with me."

"Yeah, but you didn't invite the moth in. Besides, if the bat was already inside . . ."

"I wouldn't be likely to be too friendly to a bat, would I? I certainly wouldn't let it get close enough to bite me! If vampires can turn into just about anything, the bat could have become a moth. And

113

remember the screen—my taking it out. Tim"—
Sarah looked very serious—"once you've been bitten, you—you start changing into a vampire. Look
at Emily; she's changed a lot. I don't know how
long it takes, but I've been bitten at least twice.
And you and Jenny—you've each been bitten once,
I guess."

"Wait," Tim said, his head still reeling. "Let's go
back to the beginning. We asked the exterminators
into the house . . ."

"Yes, and they got rid of the bats—real bats, I'm
pretty sure. But remember the little one we found
in Mom and Dad's room. Remember how Tink
wouldn't go in? Domestic animals, it says in one of
these books, are terrified of vampires. I think that
little bat might have been the exterminator who
stayed behind, if one of them did. Anyway, I'm
pretty sure the exterminators—um—the vampires,
I guess I should say—brought them here, you know,
to make us call them. Look at how we found that
business card stuck in the door. And remember that
it was the same night they were here that I first
saw the butterfly."

"But you saw lots of butterflies!" Tim tried not
to think of how Tink had acted around Mr. B.

"I know. I don't understand that part, except remember that Emily saw lots of rabbits the first time.
Maybe it's some kind of magic, or maybe vampires
can control animals. I haven't actually found that
in a book, but I know that Dracula controlled

114

wolves. The vampires could have sent me the butterflies and Emily the rabbits to soften us up, to make sure we'd let the one vampire butterfly or vampire rabbit in when the time came. Anyway, one of the butterflies must have been the exterminator who stayed in the house, and he must've bitten me. And then the next night, the luna moth came, and I'd have let it in, too, if you hadn't stopped me."

"The red spot on your sheet," Tim muttered. "Oh, good grief!"

"What red spot?"

"That first morning, there was a reddish brownish spot on your sheet. I thought it was from one of your butterflies. You know, when you pinned it to your collection, or when you killed it or something. But it was your blood." He choked a little on the words.

"I shall never," said Sarah dramatically, "kill another butterfly."

"What—what about Mr. B?" Tim asked. "Tink was weird with him, yes, but no one invited him in."

"No one had to. You've been going to *him*. Anyway, now that Mr. B's bitten you once, maybe you *will* let him in."

"No way," Tim said disgustedly, feeling betrayed.

"You say that now. But remember they sort of put spells on people."

"I wish John were a real magician. I wish there *were* real magicians."

"Maybe there are," said Sarah, "since there seem to be real vampires. But if there are, we don't know any. Still, maybe John can help. He's the only one of us the vampires haven't gotten."

"You keep saying vampires, plural. How many do you think there are?"

"There's Mr. B," said Sarah promptly. "And the exterminators, like I said. Remember how Tink growled at them? So there are three at least."

"Unless one of the exterminators was Mr. B," Tim mused, thinking back to the day the van came. "We never saw the younger guy's face, remember? And now that I think of it, he sort of talked the same way. And the phone number!" He clapped his hand to his head, then ran into the kitchen and got the white card, which they'd stuck on the refrigerator. "Yes," he said, trying to keep his hand from shaking. "It's 555-9872. I think that's the number Mr. B started to give me when I asked him how I could reach him. Sheesh, Sarah, what are we going to do?"

"I don't know. Get some garlic, I guess, to start with. Vampires hate garlic; it repels them."

"Have we got any?"

"No. I already checked. And there isn't any in the garden either; Mom doesn't grow it. So we'd better get some tomorrow—lots—and tell John to get some, too. And let's all sleep down here tonight. Maybe if we're all together, we can put up a fight, or even confuse the vampires. Remember, you and Jenny are stronger than I am, more—more human, too. You might have to tie me up or something."

"Oh, come on! You sound human enough now. I'll get the sleeping bags."

"And I'll get Jenny."

About half an hour later the three Hoskins children were lined up in their sleeping bags on the Big Room floor, with Tink snuggled next to Tim. They'd tried to have him lie next to Sarah, as extra protection, but he seemed to prefer Tim—which, Sarah said in a calm voice that Tim knew was a brave cover-up for terror, "just proves that I'm beginning to be a vampire already." Jenny was in the middle, since she was the youngest and since Sarah said she was afraid it would take less time to "vampirize" her, since she was so small.

For a while, everything was quiet in the cabin. But Tim couldn't sleep; he lay there listening to his sisters' breathing, and his dog's. He couldn't stop thinking about all those bats, both in the house and on Spool Island—why there?—and about Emily and Sarah and Jenny and the little kids at the parties. Were they all doomed to die and become vampires, as Sarah had said? Was he doomed himself? He shuddered, thinking of a vampire version of Emily, and one of Sarah, each clad in a long white gown, her teeth long and pointed, her eyes cruel and cold—cold like Mr. B's as he'd bent over Tim, having just sucked his blood . . .

I certainly won't let him coach me anymore, Tim thought, that's for sure!

There was a soft whooshing sound outside, like a gentle wind, and Tink raised his head, growling softly.

"What is it, Tink?" Tim muttered. He hadn't realized how sleepy he was, how very sleepy, and weak, too, from the blood he'd lost, probably, and from the near drowning . . .

Tink leaped to his feet, went to the porch door, threw back his head, and howled.

Oh, no, Tim thought, snapping to attention. They're here!

He struggled out of his sleeping bag, ran onto the porch, and wrenched the door open. Reeling, he went outside, just in time to see mist swirling in the moonlight. When it cleared, a bat swooped down from a tree. It grew huge before his astonished eyes and then became Mr. B, smiling, his teeth long and horrible. Behind him was another giant bat, and a third one behind that.

"Good evening," said Mr. B with a sinister smile. "Good evening, my young athletic pupil. I have fed, as you may remember, but my friends have not. So if you will excuse us . . ."

Tim felt his eyes widen as the two figures behind Mr. B changed shape and color. The black wings of the first bat became white fur; its bat legs and bat ears became rabbit ones. The other bat's black wings became green; its beak became an insect's long proboscis, and its bat ears became antennae—the luna moth! It flapped its wings gently, sailing toward the house.

"NO!" Tim shouted. "Tink—get it!"

But Tink was cowering in one corner of the porch, shaking and whining. His front legs looked as if they wanted to move forward to attack, but his back legs stayed rigidly in place.

Tim leaped forward at the green moth, who turned into a person—the older exterminator. The rabbit became a really rather nice-looking lady—but her teeth were long. She smiled and said softly, moving toward him, "Do not be afraid. We are not here to hurt you. We like children. It is just that we are lonely for them, so very lonely—"

"Tim! Look away!"

It was Sarah, screaming from inside the house. "Try to look away—don't let her see your eyes. Don't look at hers!"

But it was too late. He'd already looked, and he felt himself helplessly sinking, sinking . . .

And then suddenly, with a horrible gurgling screech, the lady became a bat again and flew up into the air, and the older exterminator did the same. Mr. B's outlines melted into mist, and all three creatures vanished.

chapter 15

Plans

"So you are a real magician after all," said Sarah to John as all four of them sat sipping hot chocolate in the Big Room a few minutes later.

"No," said John. "Emily told me about your talk, though. And I remembered from the movies that vampires are afraid of crosses, so I just held up a couple of sticks, and I guess that chased them away."

"But how did you know to come here?" asked Tim.

"I didn't, really. But I couldn't sleep after Emily and I talked, and I'd gone outside because I wanted to see for myself if a vampire really did come for her. I had the sticks all ready to hold up if I saw one. And when I was outside waiting, I heard Tink howling, so I came running over. I'm glad I went through the woods instead of by the road. I was just in time, I guess."

"Yes," said Tim. "Just in time. Thank you. This might be the best magic trick you ever did!"

"Emily!" Sarah said suddenly. "She's unprotected."

"Oh, my gosh," said John. "You're right! I better get going!"

"Garlic," Sarah called after him. "If you have any garlic, make her wear it, and rub it around her window."

But the next day, when they went to the Gibsons', carrying bunches of garlic they'd bought in the village as soon as the stores opened, they learned that the vampires had already attacked by the time John got home. When John took Sarah and Tim into Emily's room, leaving Jenny and Tink downstairs with Mrs. Gibson, Emily pushed them away, snarling like an angry dog.

"Look at her teeth," Sarah whispered to Tim.

"I know."

Emily's teeth were long and pointed, and her eyes were cold and glittering as she watched them suspiciously. Her face was almost as pale as the white sheet she lay on, and although she was weak, she recoiled from the garlic violently. Her eyes flashed furiously at them whenever they came close with it.

Tim went to the window and began hanging bunches of garlic there, but John pulled him back, saying, "It's no good. She already threw away the garlic I put there when I got home last night."

"She's so changed," Sarah whispered, watching Emily. "I don't see how she was able to touch the garlic, since she's so close to being a vampire already."

"She didn't touch it," John explained. "She opened the screen and poked it out with a tennis racket, I think. At least the screen was open and the tennis racket was lying on the floor when I came in early this morning."

"I've got an idea," Sarah said. "Let's rub garlic juice on the frame. She can't get rid of that, and we've got to do something." She reached for the bulb of garlic Tim held out to her, but dropped it with a cry of pain. "It burned me!" she exclaimed.

"You will be one of us in a while, Sarah," said Emily from her bed; her voice was strange, brittle, unlike her. Then she burst into tears and cried out in her normal voice, "Oh, Sarah, John, Tim—save me! Save me from them! I don't want to be one of them! I don't want to die and be a horrible vampire and—"

John grabbed some garlic from Tim and approached his sister with it, but Emily pushed him sharply away. "It's too late," she sobbed. "I can't help it. Something in me won't let me take the garlic, won't let you save me!"

"A cross then." Sarah picked up two pencils from Emily's desk and wrapped a rubber band around them. Before she'd moved them into a cross shape, though, she shoved them at Tim, saying, "You do it. I—I can't."

Tim fashioned a rough cross from the pencils and put it in the window—but Emily laughed and said, in the brittle voice again, "They can be mist, they can be fog, and little animals and water and fire—anything, anything. You can't keep them out."

"If they come in through the screen," John said, "they'll have to divide themselves up into little pieces."

But Emily just laughed. "Oh, you're so clever, John! You're right, they can't come through the screen, but they can come under the door if they want, or around the screen frame where it's loose. And I"—she sat up, and her eyes gleamed with an unnatural light—"I can open the screen easily; I can even take it out." Then she fell back, sobbing. "And I will, I will, I know I will!"

Tim was too horrified and helpless to speak at first, and so, he could see, were the others. But finally he found his voice and said, "What can we do then, Emily? There must be something."

Emily looked at Sarah, her eyes pleading, as if

she was begging her to think of a solution. But then they hardened, and she said, "How should I know?"

"She's much too far gone," Sarah whispered. "At least she's too far gone to help us help her."

"If we can't keep them away from her with garlic or crosses," Tim said slowly, "then I guess we'll have to—to destroy them." He looked at Sarah as John nodded in agreement. "But how, Sarah?"

Sarah glanced at Emily. "Not here," she whispered.

They left Emily's room and went downstairs.

Mrs. Gibson was working on some needlepoint in the living room, Jenny at her knee and Tink on the rug beside her. She looked up brightly as they went through, and asked, "Stay for lunch? Jenny says she'd like to."

"Sure," Tim answered, noticing too late that Sarah was shaking her head. "Sorry," he said when the three of them had gone outside.

"It's just that I'm not hungry," Sarah told him.

"Shouldn't you try to eat, though?" asked John. "To keep up your strength? I mean, you've lost blood now, like Emily . . ." His voice broke, and Tim realized suddenly what John must be feeling—what he'd feel, too, if the vampires continued to prey on his own sisters.

"I should, I guess." Sarah walked onto the terrace outside the Gibsons' back door. "But it's hard. I really don't feel like eating food . . ."

Her voice trailed off, and Tim, not wanting to think of what she might like to eat, said harshly, "Well, try. We've all got to try." He sat down in a lawn chair on the terrace. "Okay. Let's make a plan. What are we going to do?"

"I don't know." John sat down also.

"Tim's right that we've got to destroy them," said Sarah. "It's not only us, after all. It's those other kids, too, the birthday party ones."

"I'd forgotten them," John said. "You're right, though."

"But how are we going to do it?" Tim asked. "Find their graves, like in the movies, and pound stakes through their hearts? Come on!"

Sarah looked grim. "If I had to, I'd at least try it. But I think there's another way. A couple of those books I've been reading said sunlight destroys them. Just melts them away. Of course they know that, so they only go out at night. But maybe we could figure out how to get them to stay outside till the sun comes up."

"We have to find them first," John reminded her.

"Vampires," said Sarah, "have to lie in dirt from their native lands during the day. Usually in a grave or a coffin or something. So all we have to do—"

"Grave!" Tim shouted. "Spool Island!"

The other two looked at him as if he were crazy.

"Don't you remember?" he said excitedly. "The dirt in the graveyard there was all sort of scratched up around a few of the graves! We never did check to see if it was frost heaves or real digging."

"And there was that box of dirt on the beach!" Sarah added. "Wow!"

"Yeah, it figures," said John. "If those city guys who bought Spool Island were really vampires, of course they'd put up No Trespassing signs. And of course they wouldn't show themselves. That's why there wouldn't seem to be people around. Oh, wow."

"And the exterminators!" said Tim. "They fit, too. I bet that's why they weren't listed in the phone book. You were right about them, Sarah."

"I wonder," she said slowly, "if they were using our house as a cover, sort of, when it was empty. You know, when we were still in Boston. Even if they were living on Spool Island, the cabin would have been a lot more convenient for attacking Emily and those other kids."

Tim whistled. "I bet you're right, Sar'. And the bats . . ."

"The real bats," said John, "could be a cover, too. If anyone saw real bats flying in and out of your cabin, or around Spool Island, they wouldn't notice a couple of extra ones when the vampires came and went in bat shape."

"I think we've got it," said Sarah happily. "Hey, we're pretty good, you know? I think we've got all the important stuff figured out."

"Now," said John, "all we have to do is check out the island."

"And then if we're right, go back tonight after dark, wait for them to come back, and"—Sarah paused, then went on soberly—"get rid of them somehow."

There was a short silence.

"What about the dinghy, John?" Tim asked quietly.

"We're in luck there. Dad won't need it for a few days. He's gone to Boston with a load of lobsters and won't be back till tomorrow night." John stood up. "I guess it's settled then," he said, but his face looked more grave than elated. "I'll go tell Mom we want to have another picnic."

"Tell your mom we're sorry about lunch, but we'd better not stay—except Jenny," Sarah called after him. "Could you ask your mom if she'll watch Jenny this afternoon?"

"And Tink," added Tim.

Sarah nodded, and Tim knew she agreed that they shouldn't risk either of them.

We shouldn't risk *their* lives, he said to himself, trying not to add, *What about our own?*

chapter 16

Back to Spool

They had to row most of the way to the island because there was very little wind. "It better stay sunny at least through tomorrow," Sarah said grimly as they beached the dinghy and set off for the graveyard. "If it's even just cloudy at dawn, the sun trick might not work."

"How're we going to get the vampires to stay out in the sun?" asked John.

"We'll think of something," Sarah said. "And if we don't, there's always staking them."

They went the rest of the way in silence, and climbed over the low stone wall that surrounded the graveyard. Tim saw right away that the loose dirt he'd noticed before did indeed seem to mark real digging, not just frost heaves.

"I guess," said John doubtfully, "we'd better dig, too, huh? I mean, if these are the vampires' graves and they're inside them, we could just stake them now, right?"

"We don't," said Tim, looking down at the graves, "have any stakes."

"If we find the vampires," said Sarah, yawning, "we can go get some stakes. Remember, they can't be out in the sun anyway."

"Couldn't we just sort of open up their coffins then?" John suggested. "You know, just leave the coffins open so the sun can shine in?"

"No," Sarah told him. "The sun has to hit them when they're awake. You know, up and around. They're safe from it, I think, once they're in their coffins."

Tim bent to read the names on the headstones. *Whipple*, said one; *Grant, Billings*—no Biancu or Vortescu. "Look," he said, pointing that out to the others. "The names are wrong."

"Looks like a dead end," said John. Then he laughed sheepishly. "I can't believe I said that."

Sarah smirked. "Of course it's a dead end," she said. "It's a graveyard, right?"

"Ha ha," said Tim absent-mindedly. "Maybe they changed their names. Or maybe the vampires borrowed graves. I mean, their names sound like they come from another country."

"Transylvania," Sarah told him. "That's where

Dracula was from. Wallachia, actually. It's in Romania. Come on, let's dig. That's the only way we're going to find anything out."

"What are we going to dig with?" John asked. "I don't see a whole lot of shovels."

"You're right," Sarah agreed. "Neither do I."

Tim glanced around the graveyard. "There's a shed over there," he said, spotting one behind some bushes and heading for it.

Sarah ran after him, and John followed.

The door was padlocked, but it took Tim only a few seconds to unscrew the hasp with the screwdriver on his Swiss army knife. Putting the hasp carefully in his pocket along with the screws so he could reassemble the whole thing later, he pushed open the door.

The inside was shadowy, cobwebbed, and dusty, as if no one had been there for many years.

"Look," said Sarah, pointing.

In the far corner, neatly leaning against the wall, were several spades, a crowbar, and an edge cutter.

They lugged the spades out into the light and started with the grave marked *Whipple*, each digging at a different side.

After about fifteen minutes, John paused and leaned on his spade. "How deep," he panted, "do they put coffins anyway?"

Tim and Sarah stopped digging, too, and Tim

looked at the neat pile of dirt behind each of them and then at the hole they'd all made. It was uneven, but only about a foot down at its deepest. "I don't know," he said. "But aren't there poems and songs and stuff about being six feet under?"

"That's deeper than we're tall," Sarah observed, rubbing her arms.

"Then I guess we'd better get going again," John said. He resumed digging, and the others did, too.

Tim lost track of time after a while, and was only dimly conscious of Sarah and John, digging and occasionally resting beside him. He thought mostly of his aching arms and back, of his shirt sticking to him, and of the sun pounding down on his head.

Soon, in order to go on digging, they all had to jump into the hole, and then it was even harder, for they had to toss the dirt up to get it out. Tim began to feel that he'd done nothing in his whole life but dig and would do nothing else . . .

"Test bores," John said finally, leaning on his spade again. "Like the ones archeologists make when they're on a dig. If we stuck a long skinny pole down till we hit something, we'd find out if the coffin is still here."

"What do you mean, if it's still here?" Tim asked, annoyed. "Of course it's here! This is a grave, isn't it? It's got a headstone and everything, hasn't it? What else would be here but a coffin?"

"It doesn't look as if there's a coffin so far, does

it?" John observed. "We're pretty far down already. Sarah, what do you think the messed-up dirt around the graves means?"

"That the vampires got out of their graves," she said promptly. "Vampires push open the lids of their coffins and get out. Then just before dawn, they get back in."

"And cover themselves over again with the dirt?" John asked. "How?"

Sarah and Tim stared at him. "I don't know how," Sarah said after a minute.

"Maybe," Tim said slowly, "the vampires have taken the coffins out of the graves."

"Wow!" exclaimed Sarah. "I bet you're right! Maybe the vampires didn't have coffins of their own, so they had to borrow some!"

"And do what with the bodies?" asked Tim.

John glanced at the headstone above them. Tim looked, too, and saw that it was dated 1805. "I bet there wasn't a whole lot left of Mr. Whipple's body," John said. "You guys rest a minute. I'm going back to the shed to see if I can find something long we can use as a probe."

Sarah immediately slid into a sitting position and, leaning back against the grave wall, closed her eyes.

Tim sat cross-legged opposite her. He wondered how she felt after all that digging. She really did look pale; in fact, the skin around her eyes was beginning to be almost transparent. He wished he could see her teeth . . .

No, he thought, I don't. I don't want to know. The phrase "my sister, the vampire" popped into his mind and he winced.

"Here we are," came John's cheerful voice. "I'm not sure what this is"—he brandished a long, thin metal pole—"but I think it'll do. It even has a sort of point at one end."

"Maybe it's a clothes pole," said Sarah, opening her eyes. "Or"—she giggled—"a Maypole. Can't you just see it?" she went on shrilly, scrambling to her feet. "Ghosts and skeletons coming out of their graves and dancing around a Maypole, weaving crepe paper in and out, in and out, at midnight on the first of May? La la la la." She danced hysterically around the grave, faster and faster . . .

"Sarah," Tim said quietly.

She stopped. "Sorry."

John had jumped down into the grave with the pole and was poking it into the earth. "Nothing," he said after the first stab.

"Wait," Tim told him. "We ought to mark off depths, like a lead line on a boat. That way we can have an idea if we've gone far enough. Here." He took the pole. "It's supposed to be about a foot from your wrist to your elbow."

"If you're an adult," John pointed out.

"We'll use your arm then," Tim said. "You're the largest. And we'll add a little."

"Or we can use height," said Sarah. "I'm four foot ten."

Between John's forearm and Sarah's height, they approximated one-foot lengths along the pole and marked them by using Tim's knife to scratch lines in the metal, which, luckily, was fairly soft. Then John resumed his poking.

"Nothing," he said, after about a dozen sharp stabs. "Nothing—wait!" He withdrew the pole, said, "About two feet," and stabbed again. "There's something here," he told them in a funny voice.

"Stab around it," said Sarah. "Let's see how big it is."

There was nothing around it.

"A rock?" Tim suggested.

"Or a coffin buried end up," said Sarah.

"Why," asked John, "would anyone do that?"

Sarah shrugged. "Strange island custom, maybe," she said. "Who knows what they did in eighteen-whenever it was? We'd better dig anyway, to make sure."

"Here," said Tim. "Let me. You look awful, Sarah, and John, your arms must be tired."

No one objected, although Sarah glowered at being told she looked awful. Tim ignored that, took one of the spades, and carefully dug around where

John's pole had hit the hard object. Whatever it was seemed to be quite small, but it was certainly at the right depth, if they were right that their original hole was four feet deep and if the measurements on the pole were accurate. He felt the hard object move under the edge of the spade, and with a little twisting and sliding, he was able to bring it up.

They all stared at it.

"I know," said Sarah after a few seconds. "I bet it's a handle."

"From one end of a coffin," said John. "I bet you're right!"

Tim had to agree. The object he had unearthed was gold-colored metal and reddish-brown wood—an almost square, thin piece of wood, with a metal bar protruding out from it for about two inches, attached with metal brackets. The edges of the brackets were fancily fluted, and the bar itself had a few decorative knobs on it.

"So," Tim said softly, "there was a coffin here once."

"And someone," said Sarah, "dug it up. Only it was so old . . ."

". . . that one end fell off," said Tim.

"Which means," John went on, "that it can't have been very useful as a—you know."

"As a vampire bed?" said Sarah. "No, I guess

not." She glanced up in the direction of the other disturbed graves. "That means they had to dig up more graves."

"More carefully," said Tim.

"For more coffins," finished John. "Come on."

They all climbed out of Mr. Whipple's grave and went to the one marked *Grant*, where they took turns probing.

Nothing.

"So," said Tim, "they got all of this one, probably. I don't think we need a lot more evidence. I think we should look for the coffins. It's getting kind of late."

John glanced at his watch. "Yeah. It's three o'clock. But we ought to put the dirt back in Whipple's grave. We don't want to tip the vampires off to what we're doing."

"You're right." Sarah reached for a spade.

"No, Sarah," Tim said. "You look around the church and see if you can find the coffins. John and I will dig."

"Sexist pig," said Sarah. "I can dig, too."

"Sure you can." John put his hand on her shoulder. "Better than us, maybe. But not when you've been giving transfusions to vampires. You've done enough."

Sarah made a face at him, but she left, heading for the old church, and Tim and John carefully refilled Mr. Whipple's grave.

"Poor Whipple," said John when at last they'd finished and were stamping the dirt back down. "I wonder what happened to his bones."

"Maybe they just disintegrated," Tim said. "I think that's what happens when bones hit the air after a long time."

"Now there's a trick for you." John dusted off his hands. "If I could get some old bones, I could *really* make them disappear! No more wires, no more sleight of hand . . . Look, here's Sarah."

"I found them!" Sarah shouted, running toward them and waving her arms. "I found the coffins!"

chapter 17

An Unpleasant Surprise

"There wasn't anything in the church," Sarah said, leading them up the road toward the factory. "Just old pews and broken statues and a pile of something on the altar that must've been flowers once. So then I remembered the boxes you said you saw in the factory last time . . ."

"Good thinking," said John.

"And I went up there and the door was open; I guess you left it that way when you ran out because of the bats. So I looked in—and there they were." She paused with the boys at the foot of the path to the factory door and leaned on the old spool as if she needed to catch her breath. "Maybe you were too worried about the bats to notice that the boxes were . . . you know. Coffins."

"Did you actually see the vampires?" John asked uneasily.

"No," said Sarah. "I—I sort of didn't want to look. And you have to be pretty careful. They sleep in their coffins, but it isn't a real sleep. They can see you if they open their eyes. They can't do anything about it if it's daytime, but they remember who you are and they're sure to attack you that night." She paused for a minute. "Of course," she went on, "they already know who we are and everything, but if they were really mad, they wouldn't just attack to—to get blood. They'd attack to kill, I think, if they knew we were after them. So we've got to be very careful they don't know we're after them till we're ready to do something about it."

They walked quietly the rest of the way up the path and crept into the factory. Tim felt his heart beating faster than normal and he realized he was sweating again, even though it was dark and cool inside.

There was no sign of the bats, but at one end of the large and otherwise empty room were three coffins, old and battered and dusty. One was missing a panel and handle at one end.

"Sheesh," breathed Tim.

"I don't believe this," John said. "I've sort of believed it all along till now, but now I really don't believe it."

"You'd better," Sarah whispered fiercely. "Think of Emily."

"I *am* thinking of Emily," John whispered back. "And you. And Tim and Jenny and those two little kids. But I still don't believe it."

Tim cleared his throat. "Shouldn't we look in the coffins?"

"And have the vampires see us?" said Sarah. "No way. I told you what they'd do if they knew we were after them."

"Then what are we going to do?" Tim whispered. "We've got to have some kind of plan."

"Hadn't we better go outside?" John asked. "What if they hear us?"

Sarah led them out and down the path. Tim had never been so glad to see the sun.

"We could wait till dawn." Sarah sat wearily on the old spool. Her feet just barely reached the ground. "You know, wait till they come back from their nightly attack. And then we could somehow prevent them from getting back into their coffins so the sun will get them. I've read that you can make them count something—something small, like rice or grain."

"Why would they do that?" John asked.

"I don't know. I think they have to."

"Sounds risky," said Tim. "What if they don't? They must know what'll happen if they do."

"I agree," John said.

140

"Okay," said Sarah. "We can do the stake thing instead. We'll need stakes, though. And we'll have to be ready to really use them. There's no second chance, remember. If the vampires see us, they'll finish us off that night."

Tim felt the blood drain from his face. "The thing is . . ." He found himself whispering again, so he coughed and tried to speak normally. But it wasn't easy. "The thing is, they're—they're so much bigger than we are."

"But helpless," said John. "Aren't they?" He looked at Sarah.

"I think so," she answered. "Except for being able to see us. In all the books," she went on, "it says that it takes tremendous courage to stake a vampire. That's even the words one of the books used: 'tremendous courage.' "

There was a longish pause.

"Yes," said John finally. "I guess it would, wouldn't it?"

"Sure," Tim agreed. "Tremendous. I mean, there you'd be, armed with nothing but a stake . . ."

"We haven't got any stakes yet," John reminded them.

"No," said Tim, "we haven't."

"We'll have to make them," Sarah said. "All you need is a piece of wood. Ash or oak, I think, are supposed to be the best. Or hawthorn."

"There aren't any oak trees on this island," John

told them with great authority. "Or in Starfish Harbor either."

"I don't know what an ash tree looks like," Tim remarked. "Or a hawthorn."

"There are books, you jerks," said Sarah. "We can look that up easily enough. Besides, I don't think it *has* to be one of those."

"How about swords?" John suggested, pantomiming a few classy lance thrusts. "I bet swords would be good."

Tim gave him a look. "Oh, right. I'll just go sharpen up Excalibur. But," he added, "there's our probe. You know, that long metal thing."

"It has to be wood," Sarah said.

"If they can open their eyes," said John after a short silence, sitting down next to Sarah on the spool, "wouldn't they be watching while we—you know—staked them?"

"I would," said Tim, "if someone were coming at me with a wooden stake."

"I wouldn't," Sarah said. "I'd be too scared. I wouldn't want to watch. You know, like getting a shot."

"I always watch that," said John. "So I know when it's going to hurt."

"Well, John"—Sarah patted his arm—"when you're a vampire and someone stakes you, then you can watch. Come on, you two," she added. "We've got to do it. There's no point in thinking how hard it's going to be. Besides, we don't really have to look at them, not at their faces anyway, when we stab them."

"Sure." John glanced at Tim. "Pow—"

"—in the arm," said Tim. "Bam—"

"—bull's eye on the edge of the coffin," said John. "Splinters all over."

Both boys guffawed nervously.

"We'd have to look to *aim*," Sarah snapped. "But then we could look away. Or you could look and then aim, and then raise your stake, and then close your eyes so you wouldn't have to see—you know. The result."

"Blood," said John bluntly. "There's bound to be blood."

"Yes," said Sarah. "And the vampire probably screams, too—at least that's what I've read. And then it disintegrates. But"—she leaned forward— "remember this. The vampire is then *happy*."

"Oh, sure," said John sarcastically. "I'd be thrilled if someone pounded a stake through my heart. Wouldn't you be, Tim?"

"Ecstatic," Tim said. "Overjoyed."

"You would be," retorted Sarah, "if you'd been a vampire for hundreds of thousands of years and had to go around scaring people and murdering them. It's no fun being undead. I know I wouldn't want to be." She paused. "I mean, I *don't* want to be. No way do I want to be a vampire, not when

I'm feeling—you know. Normal. But I will be if we don't get rid of these guys. And so will Emily and Jenny, and you, too, Tim, and—"

"Okay, okay." Tim's mind conjured up a sudden image of himself in a flowing black cape with a red lining, like Bela Lugosi or Frank Langella in *Dracula*, sweeping into people's houses, gazing into the eyes of ravishing beauties and having them swoon at his feet. The more he thought about it, the more wonderful it seemed.

But that must have been the budding vampire part of him, for the vision slowly receded when he remembered the Iron Boy, and thought of his grandfather and his parents and Jenny, and exploring the islands in the dinghy with John and Sarah.

"Okay," he said again. "But let's practice first or something. And make a real plan. I mean, we can't do it now anyway; we've got to get the stakes ready."

They went back down to the beach, where it seemed less spooky. There they took turns lying down and pretending to be vampires while the one not lying down practiced staking, very carefully and seriously now that they'd decided what to do. *Lift stake*, Tim told himself when it was his turn and the "stake"—which they'd decided to pantomime, for safety's sake—was poised over his sister's chest. *Take aim. Close eyes* . . .

"Tim," said Sarah in a spooky voice, breaking

the solemn mood, "you do not have ze correct aim. Ze stake must be lifted directly over ze heart."

"It *is* over the heart, you jerk. Heart's on the left side. That's where you put your hand when the flag goes by."

John sat up from his "coffin," a rectangle drawn on the sand. "No, she's right, Tim. You ought to know that; you're the athlete. The heart's more in the middle, really, just a little bit over to the left." He stood up, went to Tim, and moved his hand, while Sarah closed her eyes again.

"Eef you touch my body," she murmured, "you are ze dead meat." Her eyes flew open, and she said, "Good grief! I guess I could really do that, too! I could make a vampire out of you!"

"Not yet you couldn't," Tim said grimly. "You're not one yet. And I've been bitten, too, remember that. Now shut up and close your eyes."

"No," said Sarah in her ordinary voice. "I'm going to keep them open. Partly because the vampires will probably watch us, like John at the doctor, and partly because I want to make sure you don't slip and sock me."

Suddenly Tim felt tired and sad. "Sarah," he said quietly, "I'm doing this partly for you. And I could never put a real stake into anyone. Especially"— he found he had to clear his throat suddenly—"especially not you."

Sarah's eyes softened, and she sat up. "I know, Timmy," she said. "I couldn't do it either."

"Neither could I," said John sonorously from his "coffin."

Sarah lay down again. "Stake me," she ordered dramatically through her teeth, "you fiendish human! My friends vill get you for zis. All through ze ages, zey vill haunt you, generation after generation for—ARGH!" Sarah gave an ear-piercing shriek and a very realistic gurgle as Tim, his hand stopping several inches away from her chest, said, "Bam!" He forced himself to watch as she writhed, twitched, and then lay still.

It was easier with John but no less dramatic; after all, he was used to performing.

Then it was Tim's turn to be the vampire, and it was rather fun actually, watching through half-closed eyes as Sarah's hand descended, and shrieking as soon as it stopped and she said, "Gotcha!"

Sarah looked tired again when they were finished. "Okay," she said, rubbing her eyes. "Now I guess we'd better find stuff for the real stakes."

John looked at his watch. "We better go back to the mainland for that. It's five now. Supper's at six, and if I'm late, I might not be allowed to use the dinghy tomorrow. It'll take us at least an hour to row back. There's still no wind; we can't sail."

"I wish," said Sarah wistfully as they walked toward the dinghy, "that we didn't have one more

night to get through. I'm not sure how I'll be if—
you know."

"Garlic," said Tim. "We'll use lots of it tonight.
And we'll all sleep in the Big Room again."

"That's okay for us," said Sarah. "But what about
Emily?"

"I'll think of something," John told them. "Maybe
I can tie her down so she doesn't get rid of the
garlic. Or put some kind of cross outside her window, where she can't see it but the vampires can.
I wish we could do something about those two little kids, but I guess we'll just have to count on
staking the vampires tomorrow."

"They'll be okay," said Sarah, "as long as the
vampires don't—you know—kill them. We'll all be
okay if we can manage to destroy the vampires before they finish destroying us."

They piled into the dinghy, and John took the
oars. "Now for the plan," he said, once they were
under way. "When exactly are we going to do it?"

"First thing after breakfast," said Sarah. "Your
dad will still be in Boston, right? So we can have
the dinghy?"

"Right," John answered.

"That means we really should make the stakes
tonight," said Tim.

"Or tomorrow morning first thing," Sarah suggested. "The vampires won't move till sunset once
they're in their coffins, after all, so we don't have

to hurry. We just have to get them before sundown."

"The first job tomorrow then," said Tim, "is finding stuff for the stakes. It might take a while to make them—cutting branches, whittling points, and all."

"Oh, it won't be so bad," said John. "We've got a good saw to cut the branches with. They shouldn't be thick ones, after all, or we won't be able to handle them."

"I don't think I've ever seen an oak near us," Sarah announced after a few minutes, during which John rowed silently and Tim tried not to think about what they were going to do the next day.

"I told you there aren't any," John said. "But Mom keeps talking about an ash tree she likes, so I can probably find out from her where it is."

"I hope it's got low branches," said Tim.

"We've got a ladder." John glanced over his shoulder as if to check how far they still had to go.

"So," Sarah said wearily, "we're all set."

"Jenny," said Tim. "Tink."

"Oh, good grief!" Sarah exclaimed.

"I bet Mom'll take them again," John told them, "if we say we'll be gone all day out to the islands. She knows Jenny gets tired and cranky and stuff, and you can say we're leaving Tink with her so she'll have someone to play with."

"Good." Sarah leaned back and closed her eyes.

They didn't talk much for the rest of the way, or when they tied up the dinghy and climbed onto the dock. Then they stood there quietly for a few minutes, and Tim was sure the others felt as he did: that what they were about to do was very dangerous, life-threatening even, and that no one else could do it for them—for of course, no one else would believe that their lives, and the lives of others as well, were being threatened by vampires.

"Well," said John.

"Well, I guess we're all set," said Sarah.

"Till tomorrow morning," said Tim. "First thing."

John reached out suddenly, doing what Tim had wanted to do but felt silly about: he took Sarah's hand in one of his, and Tim's in the other, and squeezed hard. "We'll do it," he said. "We'll be okay."

Tim squeezed back just as Sarah took his other hand. They stood there in a circle, and Tim felt for a moment that they were invincible.

Yes, he thought, we *will* do it!

They walked to John's to pick up Jenny and Tink.

"Oh, there you are," said Mrs. Gibson cheerfully when they arrived. "Just in time, John. Sarah, Tim—Jenny's gone home. Tink, too. Your Aunt Clara's arrived, and she came over and picked them up."

chapter 18

Disaster

Aunt Clara met them at the door. She was a tall but small-boned woman, with a hawklike hooked nose and iron-gray hair in a tight bun at the back of her neck. Usually, she wore neat tailored suits, wool in winter and seersucker in summer, gray or light blue, with a flower pin on the left lapel. But today she had on a navy-blue skirt and a white blouse, with the flower pin on the collar. Tim could see the edge of a bandage peeking out from under her skirt, and there was a white gauze patch on one side of her forehead.

Jenny was standing behind her, a mischievous look on her face. Tink, a little subdued, stood nearby.

"Aunt Clara!" Sarah smiled; she and Tim had

agreed that they'd pretend to be glad to see her. "How are you feeling?"

"Quite well, thank you." Aunt Clara hugged Sarah and kissed her cheek. "Hello, Timothy Daniel."

"Hi, Aunt Clara," Tim said, wincing a little at the hug and kiss she gave him. "How's your car?"

"The old car is dead, long live the new," Aunt Clara said cheerfully, in her usual clipped tones. "It's got a foreign-sounding name, and it's absolutely won-der-ful. If it weren't for my bumps and bruises, and leaving you poor children alone to fend for yourselves with the neighbors, I'd almost be grateful for being forced to buy it. Now come in, children, do, and wash; it's way past time for supper."

Supper, Tim had to admit, was a good deal better than it would have been if they'd cooked it themselves: meat loaf with tomato sauce, mashed potatoes, peas, and a green salad with bits of toast in it—"crew-tahns," Aunt Clara called them. For dessert there was apple pie, and though Sarah didn't touch it, Tim and Jenny each had two pieces. Tink made out well, too, for Tim managed to slip him some meat loaf after seeing that he wouldn't take any from Sarah. Then Sarah dropped some for him and shoved it to him with her foot. He sniffed it suspiciously, but he finally ate it.

"Now," said Aunt Clara when they'd all finished

and had done the dishes, "how about a picture puzzle before bed?"

"Oh, goody!" said Jenny. "A story, too? Please, a story?"

"There will def-in-ite-ly be a story." Aunt Clara went to the Big Room closet and pulled down a puzzle that Tim knew was too easy for him and Sarah but a little hard for Jenny. "Timothy Daniel, please get the card table."

"Yes, Aunt Clara," Tim said meekly, and fetched it.

"And Sarah, dear, would you please get me some paper and a pen? Before we do the puzzle, I think we should make up a schedule, don't you? You're looking a little peaked—so is Jenny. Too many late nights, I daresay."

Tim heard Sarah mutter something like "If you only knew" as she rummaged in the desk for paper and pen.

"Here you are, Aunt Clara," she said, handing them to her.

"Thank you, dear." Aunt Clara sat down regally at the card table and motioned to the children to do the same. "Now then," she said, "let's make up a timetable, like those you have in school, with slots for hours of the day and bigger spaces for activities." She drew lines on the paper rapidly—perfectly straight ones, without a ruler.

"All right then," she said, surveying her work with a pleased expression. "Six o'clock, *up*." She filled in the first space.

Tim groaned and Sarah rolled her eyes. Jenny giggled. "We don't get up till eight," she said.

Aunt Clara clucked her tongue. "Much too late. Why, half the day's gone if one gets up at eight! Now, six to six-thirty, *exercise*."

Tim brightened. "Maybe I could go for my run then," he said hopefully. "But I really need an hour." Then he remembered what they were facing the next day anyway—if they could figure out how to get away—and fell silent.

"That won't be necessary, I think," said Aunt Clara. "We'll all do exercises together, on the porch." She smiled. "I learned some good new ones at the hospital. My physical therapist teaches aer-o-bics, and she gave me a good many tips when I told her I'd be staying with you."

"Aunt Clara," Tim said firmly, "I have to train for a race. The Iron Boy Tri—"

"Timothy Daniel," said Aunt Clara with equal firmness, "specific athletic training is not suitable for a boy your age. You need gen-er-al exercise. And you need balance in your life. You and Sarah are both far too fanatic about isolated activities— although," she went on, smiling at Sarah, "butter-fly collecting is certainly a step in the right direc-

153

tion. Much more suitable than worms, unless one is a fisherman, of course. Now then." She turned back to the paper. "Half past six, *breakfast* . . ."

By the time Aunt Clara dumped the puzzle out of its box and instructed them to turn all the pieces right side up before putting any of them together, every hour of the day from six in the morning till nine at night—Sarah and Tim's bedtime, according to Aunt Clara—was carefully accounted for. There was space for a swim on nice days (indoor games on rainy ones), but it was a family swim, and Tim knew from experience that he'd be told to swim parallel to the shore so he wouldn't get too tired to swim back. He wondered, as he brushed his teeth, if he should invite Aunt Clara to the Iron Boy so she could see that he was a real athlete.

That is, he thought, if I ever make it to the Iron Boy. What if she stays all summer? What if Mom and Dad can't come back for weeks—months?

Sarah was in his room when he got there, sitting on his bed, a funny-looking necklace around her neck. Tink was lying on the other side of the room, eyeing her uncertainly.

"I wish he wouldn't be so scared of me," Sarah said, nodding toward the dog. "It's like he's not really hostile—he remembers who I am and all—but he's uneasy with me." Her eyes filled with tears. "I love Tink. I hate being part vampire like this."

Tim sat down next to her. "You won't be part

vampire for long," he said gently. "And in a way, it's good Tink's like that. I mean, we can sort of tell how much you've changed by how he behaves. I know it's awful, but I guess we can't do much about it." He fingered her necklace, which he now saw was made of string with several garlic bulbs hanging on it.

Sarah sniffed. "I kept some garlic for us from the batch we got this morning. There's even a little more left over. At least I'm not so far gone I can't go near it. It makes me feel kind of sick, but I can put up with that."

"Didn't it burn you?"

Sarah grimaced. "I used a potholder. Here." She reached into her pocket. "I made a necklace for you, too, and I already put one on Jenny."

"Sa-rah?"

It was Aunt Clara's voice, but before Sarah could do anything—like remove her necklace—Aunt Clara was in the room. Tim managed to put his necklace in his pocket.

"You need your sleep, Sarah," said Aunt Clara. "No noc-tur-nal visits. Did you know that Jenny had the strangest—Why, you do, too!" she exclaimed, reaching for Sarah's necklace. "What on earth . . ."

"It—um—it's for allergies," Sarah sputtered. "Um—Jenny and I have trouble sleeping be-cause—because—*achoo!*—we sneeze so much.

And—*achoo!*—we went to this allergist—*achoo!*—*achoo!*—who said garlic was the best thing—"

"Nonsense," said Aunt Clara briskly, pulling Sarah's necklace off. "I never heard of anything so silly. Fresh air is the best thing. You're probably allergic to dust. This house needs a good cleaning, and tomorrow we're going to give it one."

"What about the schedule?" Tim asked, trying to sound innocent.

"We'll depart from it a little. One can make oc-ca-sional exceptions to any rule. Rigidity is as bad as laxity. Now, Sarah"—Aunt Clara held out her hand—"back to bed you go. I've opened the window nice and wide, and since there don't seem to be any mosquitoes and I did notice that the screen was dusty, I'll remove it. That will get rid of some of the dust. We'll clean all the screens tomorrow. I'm sure you and Jenny will sleep won-der-ful-ly."

Tim watched helplessly as Aunt Clara led the obviously terrified Sarah to her room.

Then she came back into his room and banished Tink to the porch for the night.

Much later, when the house was quiet and Aunt Clara had gone to bed in their parents' room, Tim snuck into the girls' room and gave Sarah his garlic necklace. "Split it up between you and Jenny," he said. "Whew, it's hot in here!"

"I closed the window after she took the screen

156

away," said Sarah proudly. "Part of me tried not to, but the unvampire part won. You're right, though. It's stifling in here."

"Come into my room," Tim suggested. "We can carry Jenny in, too."

"Okay. Thanks."

They made a chair of their hands for the sleeping Jenny, and carried her to Tim's bed, where they laid her down and covered her up. Sarah insisted on dividing the garlic three ways, and luckily, Tim had some string in his room, enough for more necklaces.

"I'm not closing my eyes," said Sarah, when she, Tim, and Jenny each had a necklace. "That's all. If I don't go to sleep, maybe I can fight them off."

"I won't sleep either," said Tim. "Or maybe we can take turns. But first . . ." He broke a garlic clove off one of the bulbs on his necklace and rubbed it around the frame of his screen and along the cracks between it and the window frame.

"Good," said Sarah.

"Now," he said, "about tomorrow . . ."

"Yes. What are we going to do?"

"With that schedule," said Tim, "we'll never get away."

"I know." Sarah yawned. "I wish we could go tonight. The more time that goes by, the more tired I seem to get."

"Well," said Tim cautiously, "couldn't we?"

Sarah stared at him. "With the vampires loose? Tim, you just put garlic all over everything, but if we go outside . . ."

"We've got the necklaces," Tim said. "And they won't expect us to go to the island."

"What if they hear us? Or see us leaving? They must have ways to get around garlic. They might even be able to convince me to take the garlic off, since it's so hard for me to keep it on anyway."

"I know," he said. "I know it's risky. But I don't seem to be very vampirey yet, and John's fine. I think we'd be able to help you. Look, let's get him, make the stakes, row to the island, and—"

"The garlic," said Sarah, "should stay with Jenny."

"Some of it should," Tim agreed. "But not all of it. We know we're going to be right with the vampires, probably; we'll need it, too."

"What about John?"

"You said there's more; we'll take him some. Besides, remember we can make crosses, too. Okay?"

"I guess," Sarah said. "Okay."

"We'll take the stakes to the island and hide out till daylight, and then we'll—you know."

"Stake them when they come back."

"Right. What do you think?"

"I think," said Sarah, smiling, "that for once you've come up with a good idea, Timothy Daniel."

"The next time you call me that," said Tim quietly, "I will hide all the garlic in the world and all the crosses and abandon you to your undead fate."

"Thanks a lot. You're a great guy, you know?" Sarah stood up. "I'm going back to my room to get dressed."

"I'll get dressed too," Tim said. "Hurry up. And for Pete's sake, be *quiet!*"

Ten minutes later, Tim and Sarah, carrying flashlights and a couple of extra garlic bulbs and string for John, and wearing their own garlic necklaces, told Tink to stay and crept out of the cabin and through the woods to John's house.

A light was still burning in his window.

"Can you throw that high?" asked Sarah in a whisper as they looked up at the yellow square. "I'm not sure I can. Not after those vampire bites anyway."

"I don't know," said Tim. "But I can try." He scooped up a handful of gravel from the Gibsons' driveway and drew back his arm.

But Sarah seized it, saying, "No, wait! If you hit a lower window by mistake, his parents'll hear."

"True."

"We'll have to call him."

"Or," Tim said, eyeing a tree that stood near the house and had branches near John's window, "go up that tree and call from there. Or even throw something from there—that's it." He jammed his pockets full of gravel and swung himself up into the tree.

"Be careful," whispered Sarah. "And be *qui*-et."

"Yes, Aunt Clara, dear," said Tim.

Climbing was easy; he'd always been good at it and he was in good shape, of course, from his training. It was a hemlock tree, with fairly evenly spaced branches—like steps, Tim thought, scrambling up.

But when he reached the level of John's window, he saw the problem: the branches weren't thick enough to support his weight except right near the trunk.

Okay, he thought, I'll just have to throw stuff from here.

The first handful fell a little short.

"Higher," Sarah called softly from below.

Tim fought the urge to say something cutting back—as if he couldn't see even better than she that he had to throw higher—and let go with the second handful.

It hit the window fair and square, but there was no response from inside.

Nor was there with the third handful, and at that point he didn't have a whole lot of gravel left in his pocket.

"John," he called softly. "John." Then, desperately, he hooted, owllike, then twittered like some little blackbirds he'd once watched, and whistled like a blue jay but quietly, and mewed like a gull . . .

Someone came to the window.

"John," he said again.

"Tim?" John sounded incredulous. His face appeared, illuminated by the flashlight he held. "For Pete's sake, you sounded like a whole aviary—or is it apiary? No, that's bees. Hold on a sec . . ."

He began to lift the screen.

"Never mind that," Tim whispered. "I can't come in. The branches are too thin. Get dressed and come out. Hurry."

He saw John nod, so he scrambled back down the tree, and while he and Sarah lurked in the bushes by the Gibsons' back door, Sarah made John's necklace.

"What's up?" John asked when he arrived.

"Aunt Clara." Tim explained their new plan.

"I'll get a saw," John said without hesitation. "I don't think we should mess around looking for ash trees." He put on the necklace, which Sarah had handed him silently. "I think we'll have to assume any kind of wood will do."

"What if it doesn't?" asked Tim.

"I don't know. But, Sarah, you said you didn't think it really had to be a special kind, didn't you?"

"Yes," she answered, "but I also said it's better if it is. We're going to need all the help we can get. If it doesn't work the first time—"

"Sarah," Tim interrupted, "John's right. There isn't time to hunt for a special tree."

"There's all night," Sarah retorted angrily.

"No," said Tim, "there isn't. We have to get to the island before they come here looking for us and realize we're not in our beds."

"I think," said John, "the point is that it should be a hardwood—not pine or hemlock or any other evergreen. Maybe not alder either, because that's very soft and easy to cut. It might not be strong enough for a stake, and it might even break. Birch is kind of brittle, but there are a couple of young-ish maples right at the edge of our woods. Dad planted them because they reminded him of his favorite uncle's place in Vermont."

"Won't he mind if we saw off branches?" asked Tim.

"We're only taking three. And when he finds out why, he won't mind."

"He won't believe us, you know that," said Sarah.

"He still won't mind. Maybe not much anyway. Look, we've got to take the chance. He's my father; I'll risk it."

"Good, John," Tim said gratefully. "Thanks."

They got the saw, and in a little while had three stout branches. "We can whittle them in the boat, or when we get there," John said, and they hurried to the dock through the sleeping village.

"I don't like the look of that fog," said Tim as they untied the dinghy.

"Neither do I," John said, "but it can't be helped. Let's just hope that if they've already turned themselves into fog to get here, they won't be able to see us." He threw the bow line into the dinghy and jumped in after it. "Up mainsail," he ordered. "We're lucky there's a pretty good wind."

Sarah, who seemed to have more energy again—the excitement, Tim thought—did a little whittling while they sailed. When she took over the tiller, Tim whittled, and they managed to finish the stakes by the time they got to the island.

"So far, so good," whispered John as they pulled the dinghy up on the shore.

Sarah giggled nervously. "I wonder what the vampires will think when they find us missing," she said. "I wonder if they'll be suspicious and hunt for us."

"Maybe they'll just give up for the night," said Tim.

"Or wait around, thinking we've gone out someplace. Someplace legitimate, I mean—the movies, maybe."

"It's after eleven now," Tim pointed out as they passed the cemetery. "I think they'll know something's up—oh, no!"

"What's the matter?" asked John.

"We left the spades out," Tim said, horrified. "And that pole thing. If they've seen them . . ."

"It's too late now, probably," said John.

"Even so," Sarah said, "we better put them back. Maybe they haven't seen them."

They raced into the graveyard and threw the spades and the pole back into the shed. Then, a bit more slowly, they went up the road to the factory.

"Where should we hide?" asked Sarah.

"In the bushes?" John suggested, pointing to the scruffy-looking overgrown yews and lilacs around the front of the factory. "There seems to be room." He disappeared into the bushes. "Can you see me?"

"Nope," said Tim. "Good."

Sarah followed him behind a lilac bush. "How can we be sure that they've really left?" she asked as they settled down.

"We could go in and look in the coffins," Tim said reluctantly. "But I'd rather not."

"I'll go," John said. "Gibson the Great, the Invincible Vampire Hunter." Before they could stop him, he'd left. Tim heard the creak of the door as he opened it.

In a few minutes, he was back, looking a little grimmer than before.

"They've left, all right," he whispered. "The coffin lids are open. The inside of one is lined with satiny stuff—white once, I think, but it's sort of yellowy now. The other two are just plain wood. They don't look very comfortable."

"Is there any blood?" Sarah asked.

"No."

There was a sigh from Sarah, of relief, Tim thought, feeling relieved himself. But then why would there be blood? The blood would all be inside the vampires.

chapter 19

Stakeout

Tim was nearly asleep behind his lilac bush when he heard the vampires coming back. The sound was faint at first, a gentle whooshing again, as of soft wings beating the night air steadily, flying, flying . . .

He jerked awake, and poked Sarah. "Wake up," he said. "Wake John. I think they're coming."

"Mmm?" Sarah murmured—but then she snapped to attention and poked John, who was next to her. "John!" she said sharply. "Vampire alert."

"Huh? Ohmigosh, I fell asleep!"

"We all did," Tim told him. "But it's okay. They're coming now."

"So's morning." John pointed east, and sure enough, there was the faintest of glows there—a sort of paler dark blue, but definitely the first sign of dawn, just enough light to see by. "Still a while to go, though."

"Shh," Sarah hissed fiercely. "We'd better be quiet. We've got to stay hidden till they're in their coffins and asleep—oh!"

Her "oh" was more of a squeak, as three enormous bats landed in the factory yard. Two of them seemed to be carrying bundles on their backs.

While Tim, Sarah, and John watched in rapidly growing awe and horror, first one bat shape and then the others dissolved and took on human form. It was the same slow process Tim had seen before, beginning with a gradual blurring of outlines and a rearranging of them into human shape, so that at first the creatures were more bat than human, but slowly became more human than bat. Wings gradually changed to arms, and one of the bats with a bundle on its back reached carefully around as soon as it was able to and put the bundle on the ground.

"Mr. Vortescu," Tim breathed. "And Mr. B."

The third bat changed more slowly—it would be the lady, Tim realized—and sure enough, when the transformation was complete, there she was again, rather beautiful and quite young-looking but with the long pointed teeth and the cruel, cold eyes of her kind. She, too, moved a bundle from back to front—a smaller bundle than Mr. B's—but she kept hers in her arms.

Tim glanced at John; he was staring, his eyes enormous.

"It is only part of our goal," said Mr. B, nodding toward the bundles. "We are mostly failing, I think. Such a small part, and incomplete as it is. It is bad that someone has found that the coffins are not in the graves."

Tim prodded first Sarah and then John. "See?" he whispered. "I knew they'd have seen those spades."

"Shh," Sarah said.

John nodded grimly.

"But oh, my goodness," said Mr. Vortescu, "we have made a start, Vladimir. It is a start. Perhaps it does not matter that we were rushed. We can finish here; it will not take long. And perhaps these two will be enough." He bent closer to the bundle on the ground. "So pretty," he said. "So pretty. We will find the other ones before they find us, I think. My goodness." He looked more closely at the bundle. "Think of how this one will read aloud to us, and how charmingly she will sing. She will be such a comfort to us when she is ready."

"But the small one," Mr. B said angrily, "is a brat, and she will be crying for her mother. We should have been taking one of the little boys instead."

"I," said the vampire lady grandly, "will be the

small one's mother." She hugged the bundle she was holding, then laid it on the ground and pulled back the blankets it was wrapped in.

Tim had to clap his hand over his mouth to keep from crying out, and he did put his hand over Sarah's. He heard a hastily suppressed angry grunt from John.

For in the bundle was Jenny.

"Aunt Clara," Sarah whispered furiously. "She must've taken the necklace away and moved Jenny back into her own bed. Oh, Tim, what are we going to do? What if—what if Jenny's—dead and a vampire already?"

"She can't be dead so soon, can she?" asked John.

"I don't know," Tim said to both of them, trying not to think of the last possibility. He realized that if Sarah's theory was correct, Aunt Clara would know he and Sarah were missing. If she did, she'd probably be looking for them. She might even have called the police by now, or at least the Gibsons. And if that was true—

A rustling sound interrupted Tim's thoughts, and when he turned, he realized that John was straining to see what or who the other bundle contained. He winced, realizing who it probably was.

"Ha!" Mr. B said. "You will never be being a mother, Lady Veronica."

"We shall see," said Lady Veronica. She picked

Jenny up again and cradled her against her breast, bending over her, smiling, her long teeth gleaming.

Tim nearly jumped out of his skin.

"Steady," John whispered in his ear, barely audibly. "We'll get her back. I bet it's not too late. I bet she's still alive. Didn't you hear them say—"

"Look!" cried Sarah, almost too loudly, for Mr. Vortescu turned toward the bushes, frowning.

But then his attention returned to what Tim and the others were staring at. The larger bundle was moving, unwrapping itself . . .

"Oh, no," gasped John. "No!"

Now it was Tim's turn to restrain him, which he did with a firm hand on his arm.

Emily stood up, her hair flowing over her nightgown, her face pale but serene in the moonlight, her teeth gleaming—long, pointed—as she smiled at her captors and held out her hands to them.

"Welcome, my dear," said Mr. Vortescu, taking her hands. "You are our prize, our eldest. You will be our favorite daughter, always, and we will teach you all we know. You are young and you will be strong when the change is complete, and you will add new youth to our line, on and on, through the centuries."

"Yes, master," Emily said serenely, still smiling. She bent one knee and curtsied, first to Mr. Vortescu, then to Mr. B, and last to Lady Veronica.

Turning back to Mr. Vortescu, she said, "I thank you, master, for bringing me eternal life . . ."

John groaned and Tim tightened his grip on his arm. Emily, he figured, was so far gone the vampires had probably been able to get her to remove whatever protection John had devised for her.

". . . I will be grateful always and serve you well."

"You are not having eternal life quite yet, my dear," said Mr. B, stepping forward. "It will take one more time."

As he bent to Emily's neck, John broke away from Tim—but Tim came right after him. Sarah followed, and they all hurled themselves heedlessly at the vampires, taking them enough by surprise to tumble them to the ground.

Jenny woke up and shrieked, "Mommy!" and Tim shouted, "Run, Jenny, run away down that road and wait for us!" and Emily, with a look of terrible uncertainty, gasped, "John?" and John yelled, "Run with her, Emily! You heard him, you're not quite a vampire yet"—but Tim was too busy to see if the girls obeyed, for he was tangling with Mr. B, who, as he knew, was strong and fit and was proving more than a match for him. Despite the garlic, which obviously bothered him greatly, Mr. B was wrestling him to the ground, near the big spool . . .

—of *cable*, Tim thought excitedly, trying to signal

171

John and Sarah, and maneuvering his body so that his hand could just reach the free end of the cable. As Mr. B lunged at him, his face still averted from the garlic, Tim yanked. The end of the cable had worked out of its insulation and was badly corroded; he had a moment of horror when it broke off in his hand. But he managed to grab more right away, and this part was insulated, and held. Quickly, he pulled it across Mr. B's path—and Mr. B tripped, rolling over on the ground. Tim saw his chance then, and, whirling his arm like a windmill, he twirled the cable so it wrapped around Mr. B as Mr. B. rolled. And finally, whipping out his Swiss army knife with his free hand, he managed to open its wire cutters and, with a little effort, he was able to cut the cable.

Before he could decide how best to fasten it, John was at his side, deftly twisting and tying. "The Great Gibson knot!" he cried, his eyes shining triumphantly in the dim light. "The one that can't be untied. I'm pretty sure I've perfected it! Yes—there we are!" He stepped back, and after a quick glance down the road where Emily and Jenny had run, he bowed to Mr. B, who snarled, scowling up at him. "Gibson the Great!" John proclaimed, bowing again.

But there was no time to rejoice.

Sarah was grappling with Mr. Vortescu, who was clearly out of shape but a lot bigger than she was. He kept his face turned away from the garlic, too, and Sarah was doing pretty well, as if the need to fight had made her stronger despite the blood she'd lost; like a terrier, she was everywhere at once, punching, scratching, gouging, biting. But Lady Veronica was moving toward Tim and John . . .

Tim almost panicked, and John shot him a desperate look. But then John's manner changed and he bowed once more, saying, "Ladies and gentlemen, Gibson the Great, The Great Gibson, will now entertain you."

Tim found himself almost laughing with relief as Lady Veronica froze and Mr. Vortescu looked up, surprise and uncertainty on their faces.

"Shift!" Mr. B cried to them. "Be changing shape while you are still free and able to."

But they hesitated, their eyes on John, who, though he still looked desperate, was flapping his hands in a very professional way, producing flowers, rocks, coins, apparently out of thin air . . .

And then, behind the vampires, Tim saw an amazing and wonderful sight: Tink, Champion Tinkerfield Coreopsis—who, like all domestic animals, was deathly afraid of vampires, and who when they'd left had been sleeping on the porch—was running up the road, water dripping from his sleek body, running, running, his hackles up, the fiercest of snarls rumbling in his throat, his eyes blazing.

When he got to the factory yard, he put his head

down and charged at Mr. Vortescu, bowling him over and snarling, biting, standing on him.

In the few seconds it took for that to happen, while John kept on with his magic tricks, Tim managed to maneuver the spool behind Lady Veronica. He handed Sarah the free end of the cable. She nodded and casually walked away, so that the cable stretched behind Lady Veronica. Out of the corner of his eye, Tim saw Mr. Vortescu try to get up, but Tink held him firmly down. Lady Veronica half turned at the noise he was making, and at the warning cry that now came from Mr. B—but at that moment, Tim and Sarah pulled the cable taut and snapped it against the backs of Lady Veronica's legs like a low-slung jump rope, and she toppled.

Quickly, John ran to them and helped them tie her up with more Great Gibson knots. Then they turned to Mr. Vortescu, but by now Tink had him so terrorized that it was an easy matter to tie him, too.

"Are you all right?" Tim gasped to no one in particular.

"Yes," said John.

"Sure," said Sarah. "Oh, Tink!" She threw her arms around the dog, who was, Tim now saw, trembling like a leaf in a storm, despite his brave deed.

"He must've swum here," said Tim, hugging him, too.

"After Jenny," said Sarah. "To save her." She kissed Tink, who licked her face as if he'd forgotten she was part vampire, or didn't care. "You're the best of dogs," she told him. "Very best of dogs."

John gave Tink's ears an affectionate pull, but Tim could see that his eyes were on the vampires, who were lying still now, looking alternately at each other and at the three of them. "Can they change shape while they're tied up?" John asked Sarah.

"I don't think so," Sarah said.

"We could show you," said Lady Veronica, "how we change. It is interesting, no? Just loosen this wire a little and I will become a—a beautiful bird for you, a lovely horse for you to ride . . ."

Tink moved closer to her, growling.

"No thanks," said Tim. "We've seen all we want to see."

"We'd better find the others," John said. "Em and Jenny."

"They should be together," said Sarah. "Jenny!" she called. "Emily!"

In a moment, a small nightgown-clad figure came running up the road and hurled itself into Sarah's arms, sobbing.

"There, there, baby," Sarah soothed her. "There, kittycat. It's all right, Jenny. It's all right."

"I want Mommy," Jenny wailed. "I want Mommy and Daddy! And Aunt Clara, too. Right *now*. I don't like these scary people. I hate them."

"I know, Jenny, so do we," said Tim, brushing back her hair. "But they're all tied up now, and Tink's guarding them—look. They can't hurt you anymore. They can't hurt any of us."

"Jenny," said John, kneeling down so he was on a level with her. "Where's Emily?"

"She fell down," Jenny said. "On the beach. She"—she burst into tears again—"she won't move. She looks all—funny. Bad. Like—like them." She pointed to the trussed-up vampires, who now seemed to be talking softly to each other. Tink was standing over them, growling every time one of them moved. He was still trembling a little, but he seemed to be doing a good job of conquering his own fear.

"I'll go," said John. "If she's . . ." He ran off down the road.

If she's dead, Tim imagined he was going to say. *If she's a vampire.*

He looked at Sarah, who was still holding Jenny— but Jenny was quieter now, just crying softly against Sarah's chest.

"Sarah," he said quietly, "we have to get the vampires into their coffins so we can stake them."

"Yes, oh, yes," Mr. Vortescu called from where he lay on the ground. "My goodness, yes. Do let us get into our coffins, there's a good boy. Just loosen these ties a bit, would you, so we can walk."

"Ha!" Sarah snorted. "Do you think we're crazy?"

"My dear," said Lady Veronica, "do come here. I have a pet, right here in my dress, in my pocket. The most beautiful butterfly. Wouldn't you like it for your collection?"

"I don't think so," said Sarah coldly. "I can't imagine anything worse than a vampire butterfly."

"Tim," said Mr. B, "you know, I am just thinking of another tip for your running."

"I'll bet you are," Tim said. "No thanks. I think I can manage better on my own."

"Well, my goodness, just do let us get back to our coffins—er—beds. That is what they really are. Do not think of them as coffins. Then we will leave you alone. All we wanted was some children," he went on, sniffing a little. "We are getting old. Though our bodies do not change as we age, our hearts grow older, and we are lonely. Most vampires are adults, you know, and we miss having little ones around, as we did centuries ago when we were alive. We would be kind to you, oh, so kind, if you would let us take you."

"You would have," said Lady Veronica, "anything you wanted. Butterflies, dogs . . . Why, I brought lovely rabbits to your friend Emily. We could bring you . . ."

"Lakes, racecourses, bicycles, roads," Mr. B said. "A vampire can be going anywhere, can be becoming anything. You, Tim," he went on, "could be riding on the wind, faster, farther than anything you have been imagining before."

"No way," Tim said dryly. "Sarah, do you think we could drag them in one at a time? We do have to get them back in their coffins to stake them, don't we?" He knew that sooner or later they were going to have to get that part over with, and he knew he was going to have to bolster himself up for it. " 'Tremendous courage,' " he kept quoting to himself, and he tried to concentrate on what the vampires had done and what they were planning to do in order to expand their "family." But even then the prospect of staking them made him feel— well, sick. He looked at Sarah, wondering if she was feeling the same way, and saw an odd smile on her face.

"I'm not sure if they have to be in their coffins," she was saying. "I guess you always hear about vampires being staked in their coffins because that's where people find them. But I don't think we'll have to worry about that, Tim." She pointed to the eastern horizon, which was now decidedly pink. In fact, a small bright band, like the edge of a new gold piece, was just peeking above the line beyond the trees where sky and sea met.

"What?" Tim said, momentarily confused—and then he smiled, too. For of course now that the vampires were tied up and helpless, all he and Sarah and John had to do was wait for sunrise and the vampires would disappear.

Obviously, the vampires knew this also, for they got increasingly restless and began to squirm in their bonds, causing Tink to growl warningly again.

"I don't think I want to watch," Tim whispered to Sarah.

"Me neither," Sarah whispered back.

"I want to go home," Jenny said.

As the gold band grew wider, Mr. Vortescu babbled, "Oh, my goodness, oh, my goodness," over and over again, and Lady Veronica stared at the horizon, as if measuring the amount of time she had left. Mr. B closed his eyes and lay there silently.

Tim and Sarah turned away with Jenny. Tim started to call Tink, but decided they should leave him to guard the vampires till the sun had done its work. Then Lady Veronica called, "Children."

Tim turned. Lady Veronica was looking full at him, and her eyes were less cold now, almost human.

"You are right to leave us," she said quietly. "You will not want to watch. It will be perhaps a little frightening, and you have seen too much already. Had we succeeded—had you become like us—it would not have mattered. But . . ." Her voice broke slightly and she shook her head a little. "Much of me," she went on, so softly now that Tim had to

179

strain to hear, "does not want to have happen what will happen. But—but there is a little part of me, of all of us, that keeps a memory of human life and knows that this life, the vampire life, is false, is empty . . ."

"My goodness," said Mr. Vortescu. "Veronica, really!"

"She is being right," said Mr. B, his eyes still closed. "You know she is."

"So," Lady Veronica said quickly, "so we also thank you for what you will do. For—for freeing us." The sky brightened and her eyes changed, a hint of fear in them. "Go," she whispered. "Go quickly."

Tim, Sarah, and Jenny turned away, and just as the sun blazed over the horizon, John came running up the road toward them, shouting, "I found Emily! She's alive, but she's so weak we've got to make a stretcher, I think—hey, where'd they go?"

"Huh?" said Sarah.

Tim felt Tink's nose nudging his hand, and he turned and looked to where the vampires lay.

But there was nothing there. Just empty twists and wrappings of cable, still indented with their shapes.

chapter 20

Homecoming

They made a stretcher out of two of the branches they had planned to use as stakes, stringing cable between them to support a rough mattress, which they made of the blanket Jenny had been wrapped in. Emily didn't move or speak when they lifted her onto it, wrapped her in the other blanket, and carried her down to the waiting dinghy. But Tim could see that she was breathing.

"I think she'll be all right," Sarah kept saying as they lowered her gently into the boat. "Remember," she said to John, "that if you don't actually die of being vampirized, you get better."

"I sure hope so," John replied, and that was all anyone said as they sailed slowly back in the dawn.

Tim and Sarah helped John carry Emily home and up to her bed in the silent house, while Tink stayed with Jenny on the porch.

And then the Hoskinses went back to their cabin, crept cautiously up the spiral, and went to bed. It was a quarter past five, and there was no sign of Aunt Clara's having instituted a search.

Tim was too tired to wonder about that.

"Rise and shine!"

Tim started at Aunt Clara's voice and looked at his bedside clock. Six, of course. Three quarters of an hour of sleep. And now exercises. He rubbed his aching shoulders, his aching legs. Every muscle hurt; indeed, every muscle felt on fire, and he was sure Sarah must feel worse, since she was weak from all the blood she'd lost to the vampires.

Aunt Clara rattled Tim's doorknob. "Come along, sleepyhead. Heavens, what sloth! Rise and shine!" There was a loud clattering noise, and Tim realized she was actually banging a pie tin with a spoon.

He staggered into the bathroom and splashed cold water on his face. His eyes looked puffy. In fact, he thought, I look like an old man, and I was bitten only once. He examined his neck; the bites were smaller, less red. Maybe I'm just tired, he told himself.

He bumped into Sarah as he left the bathroom. "Morning," he said.

182

"Oh, no," said Sarah.

"Oh, yes." He tried out a smile. "Ex-er-cis-es. Rise and shine."

Sarah rolled her eyes and groaned.

At least, he thought, cheering up, she's getting better—for she was a little less pale.

Sarah groaned again a few minutes later when they were all assembled on the porch—Jenny looked almost herself again, Tim was glad to see—and Aunt Clara was leading them through a set of elaborate calisthenics. "One, two, three, four, *stretch*," she said briskly, doing the exercises herself as if she were their age instead of the hundred or so that Tim thought she must be. "One, two, three, four, five, *stretch*. Good, Jenny. Sarah, Tim, look alive there! My goodness, you two look awful. See what late nights and midnight pranks will do? Really! Putting little Jenny in Tim's room with that silly necklace on and hiding yourselves . . ."

Sarah and Tim exchanged a glance; Sarah rolled her eyes again, and Tim stifled a relieved laugh.

"What nonsense! It's all very well and good for you two," Aunt Clara was saying, "but small children need a lot of sleep. It's a good thing I decided to check on things before I went to bed! Now then: One, two, three, four, five, six, *stretch*.. . ."

Tink set up a tremendous barking from outside, and there was the distinct sound of a car engine.

Sarah froze in the middle of a stretch with one

hand poised over the top of her head. "That's his happy bark," she whispered.

"His welcome-home bark," said Tim. "Do you suppose . . ."

"Excuse us, Aunt Clara," Sarah said politely. She streaked off the porch and around to the front of the house with Tim and Jenny close behind.

"Mommy, Mommy, Mommy!" shrieked Jenny. And there they were, Mom and Dad, getting out of the car—with suitcases, so they were obviously home for good.

"Sorry we didn't phone," said Mom, sweeping Jenny up in her arms. "But Daddy wanted to surprise you."

"And how were the kids, Aunt Clara?" asked Dad when they were all inside again and had finished the preliminary hugs. "I'm sorry we were gone so long!"

Aunt Clara looked a little puzzled. "I didn't get here till yesterday," she said, "because of the accident." She looked accusingly at Tim and Sarah and then back at the senior Hoskinses. "Didn't the children tell you that?"

Sarah glanced quickly at Tim and crossed her fingers. "We didn't want to worry you, what with Grandpa and all."

"How *is* Grandpa?" asked Tim, wanting to know but also hoping to change the subject.

"Much better," Mom said—but she was looking

at Tim and Sarah suspiciously. "He's going home from the hospital next week. Now what's all this about an accident? Aunt Clara, are you all right?"

"I'm fine, really," said Aunt Clara. "And the children, who should have told you I wasn't here, especially since they said they would, worry or no worry"—she glared at Tim and Sarah—"were looked after by those nice neighbors of yours, the Gibsons . . ."

"Were you?" Dad asked Tim in an undertone.

"More or less," Tim said.

"In a manner of speaking," said Sarah.

"It's a long story," said Tim.

Mom sat down on the sofa. "I think," she said, "that you'd better tell it."

So they did, although not nearly all of it. How could we? mused Tim, running along the road a few hours later. Heck, I don't even believe some of it myself, although it obviously happened. He rubbed his neck and felt the two rapidly healing pinpricks on his throat that proved it. Since I'm getting better, he thought, Sarah and Jenny must be, too, and Emily, and the little boys.

He took a deep breath and lengthened his stride . . .

He flew along the road, feeling wings on his heels like whoever it was in Greek mythology.

No one could touch him now. He couldn't even hear the other runners behind him—but he could hear the crowd, clapping, roaring, shouting his name: Tim! Tim, go for it, man! Hoskins, go, Hoskins! Run, man, run! You're almost there . . .

He flung his arms wide and thrust out his chest, breaking the tape.

Just as he knew he would, come October.